Emmaline
and the
Second Summer

Emmaline

and the

Second Summer

by Britt Hampton

Illustrated by Sara Turner

A Classical Violets Book

For ordering information visit
www.classicalviolets.com.

For any inquiries contact
classicalviolets@gmail.com.

Cover and interior illustrations by Sara Turner of Cricket Press in Lexington, Kentucky.

ISBN: 978-0-9862221-2-2

For my children

who read such a quantity of books

I was compelled to pen them another.

I love you each and all so.

Prologue

The last day of the school year at the Landry Academy for Girls was not a special event. There was no party, no ice cream, no movies or games, no box of plastic prizes for the students to take home. And this suited one of the students finishing up her fifth-grade year just fine. For this girl loved quiet days. She would rather spend a day in the calm of a study hall with a treasured, antique book than in the excitement of parties and popcorn, candy and award ceremonies. She was not one to gossip or laugh at tales about her classmates, nor did she tend to share secrets or forget her homework assignments. She felt at peace in keeping rules and following reasonable instructions. She was a friendly girl, though she often found herself without a friend, unless, of course, the characters in her beloved fairy stories and folk tales could be counted as friends. To this girl, the kind princesses and wise queens, the young heroes and the ancient soothsayers, the helpful woodland animals and the foreshadowing blackbirds in the pages of her storybooks were as friends to her. Yet, she understood that these characters were fictitious. She was not one to imagine they were real, living characters, nor that she was in their world. No, she was much too practical and serious for that sort of thinking. Yet, she loved their stories, knew their characteristics, and decided to delight in the pages of the books they inhabited when she felt alone, which was often. She knew these characters well, and they were a comfort to her. It is with this young girl at the beginning of her summer break that our tale begins. Her name is Emmaline Hazeltree, and to her, good stories are the best of things.

Chapter One

Tears

Emmaline was a sensible girl. She believed there had to be a reason behind all of the things her mother did, behind the things her teachers at the Landry Academy for Girls told her to do, and there, assuredly, had to be a reason why she, Emmaline Hazeltree, was being sent to stay on her grandfather's farm for the whole summer. Emmaline held, as a deep conviction, that the world made sense, or, at least, that it ought to make sense. So why, Emmaline Hazeltree wanted to know, why must she leave the comfort of her little room with its tidy stacks of books lining the walls and go to a place full of animal noises and dirty farmhouse floors to stay with a grandfather she barely knew? She had, of course, asked her parents to explain why they made plans to send her away for two months, without so much as asking her thoughts on the matter. Their responses were short, vague, and never up for debate. And as she approached her eleventh birthday, Emmaline was discovering one of those terrible, disappointing, grown-up-ish truths: Just because there is a reason for something, that doesn't mean the children are entitled to know it. And though she fancied herself grown in many ways, she was, in fact, still a child.

When the day arrived for Emmaline to pack her pink suitcase with the nearly broken handle and tell her parents goodbye, something happened. Emmaline, the most sensible girl in her neighborhood and possibly in the whole town of Gardensport, began to cry.

"This will not do," Emmaline whispered to herself, her fingertips resting on her wet cheeks. She became quite vexed with herself. For, you see, she had made it a rule to cry only when absolutely necessary. She had cried when she fell off a fence post and broke her pinky toe; she had cried when her best friend, Susannah, moved across the ocean after second grade; and, of course, she had cried when Grandma Clara had passed away on Christmas Eve. Tears were warranted on those days, and so she had let the warm drops fall from her eyes, down her cheeks, and then she wiped them away with soft tissues every moment or so, as criers are accustomed to do. But she had never cried over a broken toy or an argument or a temporary goodbye, for that would have seemed irrational to sensible Emmaline. She had never found any use for crying over something that would soon be forgotten or remedied, and this disappointing visit to her grandfather's farm would be remedied at the end of the summer when she would finally return home to the comfort of her tidy, little space, her books right where she had left them.

Emmaline, stamping her tiny foot against her bedroom floor, began a futile attempt at halting her tears in their tracks. "What can be the meaning of this?"

Her voice was spilling out louder now, threatening to rise to an indisputably unreasonable volume.

She was growing panicked, but not because she was leaving her home, her parents, and her cat Cynthia, or because she was missing the opportunity to make friends with the new neighbor girl down the street. Emmaline was panicked because something was changing inside of her. These tears meant something was different, for what kind of girl cries over a summer trip, she wanted to know, as the drops continued to fall from her eyes? She could not say, and she was frightened to find the answer to that particular question.

Emmaline's eyes were growing a bright shade of pink and the skin around them was puffing when she closed her bedroom door and walked down the hall, where her parents sat waiting for her in the living room. Her dad was sitting in his brown, fuzzy chair, the one he always sat in and that smelled like the puffy peppermint candies he kept in his shirt pocket. His hair, as usual, was in need of a trim and was darting wildly in various directions. And her mother was seated on the floor, wearing her beloved purple, oversized sweater with the fuzzy, knitted buttons. Her back exceptionally straight, she was playing with the cat and a plastic ball that contained a tiny, silver bell. The cat would paw the floor again and again until her mother would open up her hands and free the ball from where she had been hiding it; the ball would slide onto the rug for just a moment until the cat would bat it away. And then her mother would pick the ball up again and hide it in her palms, while the cat sat waiting, pawing the floor. Emmaline had always found it curious how long her mother could be entertained with a cat's game. It had never occurred to Emmaline that perhaps her mother played this game for the cat's benefit and not for her own.

After spectating for three rounds of the bell-in-a-ball game, Emmaline decided she could stand this waiting no longer. She took in a deep, steadying breath before speaking to her parents. Though she was growing accustomed to being the punctual member of her family, she knew she was the child in this situation, and it upset the proper order of things for her to be the one to call order to the day. But, someone had to.

"Okay," she said. "Let's get going."

Her parents both looked up at their daughter's ruddy face, and they said nothing. It appeared to Emmaline that perhaps her mother had been crying, too, and it could have even been guessed that her father had shed some tears of his own, for his eyes were red, and she heard him sniffle—twice. And she knew he did not have a cold. Her father was one of those rare and proud people who claimed never to get sick and often made a big show of proclaiming this "fact" to those less fortunate people who often fall ill with coughs and sore throats.

Emmaline believed her family to be different than the families on her street, different than the families of her classmates, and different from families in her town. And she felt herself to be a very different sort of girl. She dressed differently, in old-fashioned skirts and dresses that she loved for their beauty and simplicity. Her thoughts were usually abroad in the fairy tales and history books she dearly loved. Her favorite story was "The Twelve Dancing Princesses," which she thought on often, for she dearly loved the idea of sisters and happy endings. She was not entirely certain, but she imagined most of the other eleven-year-olds she knew spent much of their time thinking about parties and phones and such. And if she was different, and her parents were the eccentric characters she viewed them as, then her family as a unit must, of course, be different from most families. And while Emmaline may have been correct about them being different in small ways, she was mistaken about the bigger ways. For her family, in reality, was not so different from other families in Gardensport, and from other families in the world she lived in. They were all a part of something much bigger than themselves, whether they knew it or not. They were all characters in a story. And it is because of this wonderful fact that Emmaline first began to see fantastical things.

Standing in the entrance of her living room, Emmaline studied her parents. Her steady and generally encouraging parents were now looking back up at her in silence. Emmaline felt a sudden heaviness around her. It felt as if there was something pushing in against them from the outside, like a force or a feeling or something she could not name or explain but that was real all the same, and it was threatening to knock them all over, sweep away their happy world, and move them to who-knows-where. It felt strange. It felt disturbingly strange. And then another tear fell down her cheek. She hurried to look out the window, grabbing onto the sill with both hands, almost expecting to see a green and violet sky threatening a terrible storm that would come down upon them like in a scene from a book. Emmaline almost hoped for such a sight, because then her dismay and confusion would, at least, have a sensible explanation.

She did not see anything out of order beyond her window. It was a beautiful day. The kind of day one expected to see on a postcard, with the sun shining and the golden wildflowers in bloom, standing tall and untouched by the breeze. There were only a few wisps of cottony clouds in the sky. She saw nothing out of order. *Nothing*, Emmaline thought, seeing her faint reflection in the window, *except me.*

Yet then, just before she turned back to her parents, just before she let go of the idea that something curious was happening to her, to her life, she saw something dark in the middle of her yard. It was a hole, just in front of where the white picket fence bordered her mother's herb garden. She would have to be nearer to see how deep it was and what, if anything, was inside it, but her eyes were sharp enough to know that is was definitely a hole, a rather large one.

She squared her hands on the window's dusty frame and pushed up, a smallish grunt issuing from her throat as she forced the old thing opened. She put one foot over the ledge; though she was a small girl for her age and not inclined to hardy pursuits, she was quite capable of climbing out a ground level window when it was nearer to her than the front door and there was something interesting to see, something she wanted to keep in her sight. As her feet landed soundly on the ground, she blinked and rattled her head a bit, as if to realign her eyes. But when she reopened them, the hole was gone! She walked to the spot where it had been, her steps slow, in case there was some sort of danger to watch out for. The grass in front of the herb garden was neatly trimmed and in place, with no sign of a hole ever being there. But she was sure it had been there moments before. Emmaline believed her eyes did not tell lies.

Looking back up at the sky, as though she was searching for an answer, Emmaline felt another tear fall from her face, and then she felt a cool and sudden breeze. Emmaline did not understand it, but somehow, she knew this would be one of the saddest days of her life. And also, one of the most important ones. She did not tell her parents about the disappearing hole, but she thought about it as they packed up the car, and she continued to wonder how it had gotten there and how it had vanished. There really was no sensible explanation. At least not one she could fathom. Emmaline wondered, for the very first time in her life, if, perhaps, some things were beyond her understanding. And as that thought floated into her mind, she heard a soft, clear voice, and it spoke a single word: *Yes.*

Chapter Two

The Golden Ring

The drive to Grandpa Hazeltree's farm took exactly five hours. Mr. Hazeltree had selected the longer of the two possible routes because he had declared it a safer, "less eventful route." Emmaline, not entirely trusting her father's sense of direction, continually referred to two unfolded maps from her seat in the back of the little, brown car with its freshly polished leather seats. Both of the maps were stained by coffee and crumpled from being stuffed in the car over years of business trips with Mr. Hazeltree, yet they each served the purpose of helping Emmaline to feel she had some control over the situation. She periodically traced her fingers over the route between her home in Gardensport to the farm in Wakeville, which was clear across the state, nestled in a whole different kind of world, full of mountains and waterfalls and foxes and cornfields. She would not be near the ocean for the first summer of her life, and though Emmaline was not exactly a beach enthusiast, on account of the stickiness of the salt water and the fussiness of the sand, she had always felt at home when driving by the shore. It was the color palette of the coast that she loved. That great expanse of water, moving ever so slightly, of blues and greens and grays, spreading to the horizon until the sky came down to meet the sea, brought her a comforting joy that she looked forward to on each drive along the coast. Emmaline did not love the ocean so much as she was used to it. And for a girl on the very edge of her childhood, familiarity is often something to cling to, for when children grow up, Emmaline was taught, it is time to set aside childish things. She had not yet decided which things in her life were childish and which things she may be permitted to hold close to her when she entered into the years of young womanhood. Her dolls must probably be left behind, she had decided. But her nightlight, she had thought, she might find a reason to keep, for that glowing, stained glass fairy really was a useful light, helping her to find her white, puffy slippers in her otherwise darkened room, and of course, helping her to see that there really was nothing to be afraid of in the middle of a stormy night.

It was nearly four hours into the car ride, when the quietness of the Hazeltree family was broken. Mrs. Hazeltree, tipping her glasses higher up on her nose, cleared her throat, turned back to look at her daughter and said, "Emmaline, there is something your father and I have to tell you."

And then, to Emmaline's alarm, Mr. Hazeltree grunted. Her father was not one to indulge in such dramatics as sound effects. He usually spoke his peace plainly and was done with it. This grunting alerted Emmaline, and her attention was quickly called away from her musings about what it means to grow up. Her parents now had her absolute attention. However, neither of them said anything.

Emmaline waited.

Mrs. Hazeltree made a movement to push her glasses higher up on her nose again, yet the blue plastic frames were already as high as they could go. Realizing her small folly, her mother cleared her throat and began to stare at Mr. Hazeltree who was, of course, staring at the road, which was at least one thing that Emmaline felt was not amiss at that moment.

"Okay." Emmaline's voice was such a whisper it could hardly be heard, yet her mother did hear it, for then Mrs. Hazeltree spoke.

"Charles, what is it we wanted to say?" She continued to stare at Mr. Hazeltree, which lasted so long that Emmaline thought her mother's eyes must have been burning from a lack of blinking.

"Emmaline, I believe what your mother is trying to say, is that she and I are taking some time. Apart, you know. From each other."

The Hazeltrees were all silent for a moment, everyone waiting. The parents waiting for Emmaline to react. Emmaline waiting for more information, but when it did not come, it was she who broke the silence.

"You *believe* she is trying to say that? Or she is?" Emmaline found herself amazed by her own impertinence. She had never been one to talk back, at least not usually, and not since she was a much younger child.

And there was the grunting sound erupting from her father again. Though Mr. Hazeltree's curdled expression was not directed at Emmaline, but toward her mother.

"I'm certain, Emmaline. Certain."

And just like that, her world began to unravel. Outside the car's windows, the bright green land was sloping upward, forming hills, with hazy blue mountains towering up in the distance. She wanted her father to turn the car around, to head back toward the ocean, back to where they were moments before, before her parents had spoken. But she was Emmaline Hazeltree, not the kind of girl who lived in a fantasy world or who let her imagination run wild, and so she reminded herself, *We cannot go back in time…we cannot*. As soon as she thought those words to herself, she felt a shiver run through her arms, popping up goosebumps and making her feel fitfully uncomfortable. She rubbed her hands up and down her arms, warming them and rubbing away the tiny bumps. Something felt wrong. Of course it did not occur to her that the strange feeling of wrongness came after thinking that she could not go back in time. She thought everything felt strange and cold because of the news her parents had just shared with her. This was a sensible conclusion a girl in this situation might make. However, not everything in a story is sensible, and, perhaps, Emmaline would soon learn that things were not always as they seemed to be. But, for now, oblivious to that possibility, Emmaline continued to look out the window as they moved higher up into the mountains.

"I miss the ocean already." And tears pooled in her eyes, preparing to fall down her cheeks. This time, she found their appearance absolutely reasonable. She did not try to stop them from coming, nor did she wipe them away, but she turned her face away from the mountains and watched as the teardrops fell from her face and down onto her yellow dress. Emmaline watched the droplets soak into the fabric making dark spots, with her head hung down low and her dark hair like a curtain around her, she hid herself from the pain she knew to be in the seat in front of her, but there was no hiding from the pain she felt in her heart. And the little, brown car kept on down the road.

When the Water Trails Farm sign came into view, Mrs. Hazeltree turned around and patted her daughter on the knee. "Look, Sweetie. We're here. Your grandfather's nice, little farm. Do you remember that old wooden sign hanging up there? You used to love pointing it out when you were little."

"Okay," Emmaline said, because she was not inclined to come up with a better response.

"Okay," her mother whispered back.

"You'll like it here, kid," Mr. Hazeltree said. Emmaline, hearing that his voice had a half-smile behind it, could not bring herself to smile back, not even halfway.

And then he stopped the car, right in the middle of the dirt road, below the hanging, wooden sign. He turned around and said, "Your job this summer is to have fun. Have an adventure. Try not to be so sensible all the time." He laughed a little under his breath. It was an odd, shaky kind of laugh, as if he pushed it out, trying to be light-hearted, but it didn't fall naturally from him. *Forced laughter is such a sad thing to hear*, Emmaline thought, and she found herself wondering if a forced laugh was sadder even than sobbing. "We just wanted you to know what's going on, so you wouldn't spend your time this summer wondering why we brought you here. We need to figure out some grown up things, but we want you to have a great summer, not a boring old summer around us. There is so much to do around the farm, and your grandfather is looking forward to spending time with you. Like I said, your job this summer is to have an adventure." He was rambling, which was rare for him. It seemed everything had changed at once, even her father.

Emmaline nodded, her trembling lip threatening to give way to a fresh outburst of tears, but then her dad nodded back at her, and that little nod seemed to bring her back to her usual, collected self, even if just for a moment. She decided to trust her parents.

Things happen for a reason, she said to herself. The thought comforted her. Yes, she thought, she could choose to have a great summer, have an adventure even, because then her parents would be free to sort everything out at home, and then she could come back to her room and to her books at the end of the summer, and everything would be back to normal, everything would be just as it should be. *Things would make sense again*, she told herself, *they would*.

Her dad began driving again, along the dirt road, and Emmaline saw the tall man who was her grandfather standing on the front porch. His hands in the pockets of his denim overalls, his chin lifted up a bit as he looked into the car and fixed his eyes upon Emmaline. The car stopped. Her grandfather continued to stare at her from his broad front porch, and Emmaline took in a determined breath as she stepped out of the car.

"Hello, dad." Mr. Hazeltree's voice was much stronger and clearer now than it had been before.

"Son," her grandfather said back, not unkindly, but not cheerfully either.

Emmaline's parents left within the hour. They apparently wished to allow Emmaline to get started with her summer plans right away. One might suppose that they were a bit uncaring, delivering this heartbreaking news, then dropping her off, and quickly rattling away in their car. Emmaline had not yet learned from experience that, sometimes, people can hurt you, even when they try their best not to. However, Emmaline had learned that her parents loved her. She trusted that they still did. And, it just might come to pass that in bringing Emmaline to spend the summer with her grandfather, they had started a chain of events that would mend many things which had once been broken.

Emmaline watched them drive away, and while she could not see their faces as they rode into the distance, it can be guessed that her parents watched her in their rearview mirror, quietly hoping their daughter would have a lovely summer.

Her grandfather had not yet said one word to her, which did not make her more uneasy, for she was so uncomfortable in his gruff, stern presence that she believed too many words from him would leave her in a nervous mess. He had stood to the side and watched on as her parents had hugged her and said goodbye.

But then, as soon as the front door to grandfather's house closed behind Emmaline, her grandfather walked up to her, reached into his shirt pocket and took something out. He held it out to Emmaline in his large open palm. It was a beautiful, golden ring with a large, square gemstone, the color of the sea, all gray and blue and green swirled together. Emmaline looked down at it, more amazed by its beauty than confused as to why he was holding it out for her to see. She had never seen such a beautiful piece of jewelry or such a large gemstone. It looked like something that had belonged to a queen, something one of the characters in her beloved fairy tales would have worn. As if in answer to the question in her mind, her grandfather finally spoke. "It belonged to your grandmother."

And then Emmaline pulled her gaze away from the beautiful ring to look up at the towering, old man standing in front of her, for though his extreme height, furrowed brow, muddy boots, and white hair were altogether intimidating, his voice was tender and broke a little when he spoke the word "grandmother."

He cleared his throat, then said, "My mother, your great-grandmother, gave it to her as a gift. To welcome her to the family. It's a family heirloom, passed down for generations. And you are to have it. That was what she told me. All I know is what I was told, and I was told you must have it."

She continued to look up at him, not sure of what to say or what not to say, and then he came to her rescue, for he spoke again before the silence became awkward.

"Take it," he said. "It's yours."

Emmaline Hazeltree stood perfectly still, for certainly he was joking, assuming such a serious old man could make jokes. She did not believe this exquisite ring could ever belong to such a young and unremarkable girl as herself.

"Take it." His voice was louder now, apparently ready to bring this tender moment to a swift conclusion, urging Emmaline's hand forward to take the ring from his waiting hand. She held onto the gold band with two shaky fingers, still too cautious to touch the sparkling gemstone.

"Good." He said, looking down on the ring in her hand. "She said you'd know how to make it work."

"Make it work?" Emmaline asked, but her grandfather only nodded.

"Supper's in a bit," he said, walking away down the hall toward the kitchen. "If you're still here, then I reckon I'll see ya at the table."

Emmaline was left standing in the front room of her grandfather's farmhouse, all whitewashed wooden walls with sturdy and worn furniture and soft lamplight, a little girl with dark hair and a bright yellow dress, pondering the mystery of this majestic ring that was in her hand. "How does one make a ring *work?*" And just like that, Emmaline Hazeltree, holding onto the golden ring with the sea-colored gemstone, disappeared.

Chapter Three

When We Get There

Emmaline was no longer in her grandfather's farmhouse. She was no longer anywhere, as far as she could tell. She saw nothing, only darkness, not even the faint glow of a fairy nightlight. But, the darkness was not frightening or cold. It was rather warm, and Emmaline felt cozy somehow. Something impossible was happening, and yet, she was not afraid. She felt the kind of feeling she had often experienced after eating her favorite meal: her mother's homemade chicken soup and crackers with salt crystals on them. She felt like she was satisfied and full and home, though she was surrounded by nothingness, by the darkest night she had ever seen. *It is not even nighttime*, she thought. *Or, possibly it is night.* Her mind felt muddled and full of swirls. There really was no way for her to know where she was or when she was, for that matter. It was silent in the darkness. She felt that perhaps she was moving, floating possibly. And just when she decided it did not matter if she was moving or not, for either way she felt like she was exactly where she was supposed to be, the darkness was broken by a bright, warm burst of light, and Emmaline Hazeltree saw where she was. She saw everything.

Scenes from her life were playing on the wall in front of her, all of the things she loved, all of the people she knew; they were all there, moving from one scene to another, moving back and forth in time as if her life were a movie being presented in front of her. She was in a stark, white room, the brightest white she had ever seen, as if the very walls were made of light. And there was nothing in the room, no one, only her life moving in front of her: a moving picture of her mother, playing the plastic ball-and-bell game with her cat; her classmates at the Landry Academy for Girls standing in a long, perfectly straight line in their navy skirts, waiting to enter the empty cafeteria. And then she saw her grandmother, old and tired and clutching her purple quilt up to her neck as she lay dying in her bed. The scenes moved quickly and the pictures were so vivid and clear, just as she had lived them. Emmaline turned around and looked over the room, looking for someone, or for some machine that was projecting the images. There was nothing. There was no one. And now her favorite dress shop was showing on the wall, a small, stone building in downtown Gardensport full of pastel dresses and sweaters to match. She saw her mother paying for a dress. She saw her father waiting in a chair in the corner of the store, pondering a crossword puzzle as he tapped the paper with a pencil, and then, the best sand castle she had ever built suddenly appeared on the wall. She could see the chipped shells she had decorated it with, and then she saw the little boys descending on her castle, trampling it thoroughly, and running away. She didn't hear their laughter. The room was silent. Susannah, who had been Emmaline's best friend, emerged on the picture show in front of her, with her two, golden braids, reading from Emmaline's favorite fairy tale book and pointing to a picture of twelve princesses. Susannah's picture faded away, and suddenly there was her grandfather; he was a slightly younger version of the man who had just given her the ring, with brown hair and an ironed shirt, and then the pictures began to move even faster, melting in to one another. Mom, dad, Susannah, grandma, Mrs. Sloan from school, the neighbor lady, her parents sitting in the front seat of the car as they prepared to tell her they were splitting up the family, the preacher at the church downtown, Mrs. Lindy who worked at the shoe store and wore bright cherry-colored lipstick, Emmaline's room with her stacks of books, her piano teacher, her mother's herb garden. She was mesmerized, and then the show was over. The peculiar warmth she had felt started to fade away, as if a spell was lifting, as if her mind had been covered over in a comforting fog, and now she found herself looking around. Her heart was pounding faster and faster and it seemed to be moving higher and higher, and she saw someone standing in front of her, a girl dressed neatly, in a bright blue dress that touched the floor. It was her dear friend, Susannah. She looked different, more serene and formal than the jubilant girl she knew, but there was no mistaking her kind, familiar face. Susannah said only two words, and though they were sweetly spoken, they did not do anything to calm Emmaline's panic. "Welcome home."

"I don't understand," said Emmaline. "Where are we?"

"This is your Place of Stillness. Between your life and your work."

Emmaline spoke quickly. "But, how did I get here? I don't understand. How did you get here? I haven't heard from you in so long. Your letters stopped. Now, we're here in this...this place, I guess...I don't understand."

"It is okay. Take a deep breath. First, know that all is well. Do you understand this one thing? That all is well?" Susannah smiled.

Emmaline shook her head, partly because she did not know that all was well, but mostly, the very sensible Emmaline shook her head because her sudden disappearance from her grandfather's farm into the darkness and her reappearance into this "Place of Stillness" with a friend she hadn't seen in ages—well, it just didn't make sense. Emmaline began to dwell on Susannah's words, "Place of Stillness." This strange detail—referring to such a bizarre location as a "Place of Stillness"—amidst all the other fantastic occurrences on this day, was almost too much for Emmaline to bear, and she spoke to herself, *This is not my Place of Stillness. This is some other world that cannot actually exist, and either I am dreaming or I am awake and everything I thought I knew about life is changing right in front of me, in which case I refuse to cooperate. And I insist on being returned immediately if that is the case! But, surely, I am just dreaming.* There was a third option, a scarier one, Emmaline thought for a moment, but she decided not to consider it further.

Susannah reached out and touched Emmaline's hand, prompting Emmaline to turn her hand over, open her nervously clenched fist and reveal the ring she had forgotten she was holding. Susannah plucked the ring from Emmaline's trembling hand and smiled, a sigh escaping her lips as she slipped it on her own finger. "Your grandmother had fabulous taste in jewelry, Emmaline," Susannah giggled, and it was just the laugh Emmaline remembered hearing from her a thousand times before as the two of them had made paper chains and told riddles in the neighborhood park. "Don't you think this is a beautiful ring?" Susannah was just chatting along, Emmaline thought, as if this was a normal situation, as if the two of them were not in some fantasy realm, transported there by some mysterious force. It really was enough to make Emmaline's mind spin.

Emmaline placed her hand on Susannah's shoulder and her friend looked up from the ring and into Emmaline's eyes. Emmaline finally wondered that third option aloud. "I'm dead, aren't I?" Emmaline had read about different afterlife stories from her books about ancient mythologies. She remembered that some had seemed much more agreeable than others and was looking hopefully to Susannah for a sign that this "Place of Stillness" may be on the nicer side. Emmaline waited breathlessly for Susannah's answer, and in the quiet, she heard the beating of her own heart, which she could not hold back, and in that moment, Emmaline knew the answer to her question.

"No." Susannah's face grew serious now. "Neither one of us is dead. This is no place for the dead. This is a place for children like you. You are one of the storysmiths. And I am a guide—your guide, to be exact. I'm here to help you. I always have been."

A flurry of thoughts and questions flocked into Emmaline's mind. The question that mattered the most to her seemed almost beside the point. Emmaline wasn't fixed upon what a storysmith was or how her friend came to be a "guide" or whatever she was, but rather, Emmaline's heart focused on one other question in particular. "So, you weren't really my friend? All that time when I thought I had found a true friend, when everyone else ignored me or mispronounced my name on purpose, you were just sent to Gardensport to pretend to be my friend?"

"No," Susannah's voice was clear and soft—a whisper, but with strength behind it. "That's not the way of it." She smiled, splendidly calm. Susannah took a deep breath, and motioned for Emmaline to sit on one of the two white chairs that had suddenly appeared in the room. Susannah had the air of someone who had complete confidence in how the conversation would play out, for she did. Susannah knew things. She knew she could rely on someone else to make the plan in the end. And this knowing gave Susannah a great ease to her manner of thinking and talking. The story that Susannah was a part of had an author, and she was not that author. Susannah took great comfort in this. And soon, so would Emmaline.

"Let's see. First," Susannah breathed out the word, as someone does who is about to begin to tell a tale, and then she neatly crossed her ankles and adjusted the sparkling pink bangles on her wrist, before continuing, "I was sent to you. To be your guide and your friend. But, I was also your friend because I wanted to be your friend. People often try to see things in some sort of neat, chronological order. As in, *first this happened, so then this happened.* And while that is often the case," and here Susannah leaned in a bit and whispered in an excited little voice as children tend to do when they have the best and happiest secrets to share, "sometimes, time turns and twists around itself, so that different events, different people from different times, with different ideas, can swirl together to make a better story. And when this happens, things can really get interesting."

"I...see...or, I do not, really." Emmaline leaned back a little, hoping Susannah's words would make better sense once she gave them a moment to process.

Susannah laughed, a soft, happy laugh.

"It's okay that you don't see it all now, Emmaline. It's good just to see a little bit for a start. Just know that it is possible not only that I was sent to befriend you, but also that you and I decided for ourselves to be friends. There is an author of this great story. And that story is being written and coming to life in countless different ways all at once, and the great story has a purpose. And the author can see the whole story playing out over and over again, backwards and forwards. And the author can mix chapters and characters and places and times together and can write and rewrite again and again to see the plan come together."

"The author...?"

"There is an author, or a writer, a story-crafter. There are many names for the author, but yes, there is an author here. There is an author of every story. You know that, Emmaline. And your life is part of a story, which means someone had to write it."

"We're in a story…"

"Yes, Emmaline. That's what I've been trying to tell you. We are in a story. Our world is a story—a good one. And that is why you are here. For the story."

Emmaline was silent and confused. She didn't know what to say, what to think. Everything seemed so impossible, and yet, she felt excitement spark in her mind at Susannah's words. For Emmaline was a girl who dearly loved a good story. And, sitting there, next to her dear friend, she wanted immensely to know what would happen next in the story.

"Can you tell me more? I mean, what's supposed to happen?" Emmaline asked, her voice shaky.

"There is a purpose for you, Emmaline. This world—and yes, we are still in the world you know, Emmaline, just in a different sort of space within it— has a story. The story has all been written, and it is the greatest of tales, so many twists and turns, so much triumph, so much heartbreak, so much adventure, so much everything, Emmaline. Everything!" This last word, she spoke with reverence and joy, and it made Emmaline sit up a little straighter, as she awaited the rest of this revelation.

"And this story is woven together in countless ways. Countless, Emmaline, like infinity." Susannah removed the ring from her hand and held it back out to Emmaline. Emmaline, of course, not being in any sort of position to resist, took the ring, letting it sit on her lap, not sure of exactly what she should do with it.

"And one of those ways the story is woven together is by the deeds of storysmiths, like you."

"Storysmiths." The word sounded clumsy to Emmaline, spoken by her own voice, as she did not say it with the certainty and appreciation that she heard in Susannah's voice.

"Yes, storysmiths: children who move through time, helping the story happen as it should. You have a very important job to do, Emmaline. And we must get you started quickly."

And then the white room was pulled away from them, the same way a curtain is pulled back to reveal something that had been behind it all along. They were standing in front of a long and narrow bridge, made of smooth stones, which connected two towering mountain peaks that plunged straight up from a vast ocean and into the sky. The bridge was long and beautiful, as though it had been made with great care and skill, but it was free of cords and bolts and beams, making it appear a natural part of the landscape, like an elegant rainbow of stone through the sky, bridging the two peaks that faced one another across the swirling waters.

"If you cross this bridge, then you cannot turn back. You will accept your place with the storysmiths. You will go home eventually. And you will arrive in the moment you left. For there is no escaping your own time. You will miss nothing there. And no one there will miss a moment with you. But you cannot return the same way you came, and you will forever be marked a storysmith. And that is not something to take lightly. It's a wonderful adventure, and yet, a heavy responsibility."

"And if I don't cross this bridge?" Emmaline asked, not certain she wanted the answer.

"Then you don't cross it. You go back to your grandfather's living room and eat supper." Susannah kicked Emmaline's shoe lightly, the way she used to kick it beneath their shared table in art class. "And someone else will cross here. The work will be done. It's up to you whether you'll be part of it."

Emmaline turned away from the long, stone bridge and looked at Susannah, wondering what her role was in all of this. She was a guide, but what that meant was a mystery to Emmaline. Susannah was something different, something magical or powerful or otherworldly. As Emmaline thought on this, Susannah stood silently, waiting for her friend to choose her path, to accept her calling as a storysmith or to turn it down and go back to her grandfather's farm. When Emmaline did not announce her choice after a rather long silence, Susannah spoke once again, hoping to encourage her friend to choose something, for the Place of Stillness had disappeared and they now stood at the end of the stone bridge: a place for choosing, not for being still. As it is widely understood, the edges of stone bridges are for taking momentous steps into new adventures. There is nothing patient or insignificant about standing at the edge of a stone bridge across the sky.

"It's like you have always said, Emmaline. *Things do not simply happen.* You make the choice that you will. Either way, the story will play out as it should. But you must decide, and now is the moment to decide. Will you do the work as only you can? Or will someone else do the work?"

Emmaline Hazeltree took in a deep, yet shaky breath, exhaled with some exaggeration, and then, turning to Susannah with her golden braids, she said in the steadiest voice she could master, "You and I both know what I'll do." And Emmaline, finally feeling connected to the path before her, stepped onto the bridge.

Chapter Four

The Second Summer

Before Emmaline could cross the stone bridge that would take her on her first adventure as a storysmith, she turned to her friend and said, "It was really good seeing you again."

"I'll be here, waiting for the next time you come to your Place of Stillness. That's my job as a guide: to help you sort through this calling of yours. There is no instruction manual for the children called to be storysmiths."

"Why are children storysmiths? Why not just grown-ups?"

"*Only* children are storysmiths, Emmaline, never grown-ups. Many can't be trusted to do the task set before them without making up their own plan. Children often make mistakes, sure, but they are great at enjoying the work of another without trying to make it better at every turn. Children are wonders at trusting a good author to weave a good story. There will be times when you are confused and you feel lost, even when you remember that the story has a plan. In those lost moments, you may ask questions, to the sky, to your heart, or to me, though that does not guarantee that you will receive an answer. Remember, this is not your own story. We are all a part of it, yet it does not belong solely to us. It may sound as though I am speaking to you in riddles, but please remember my words and know that everything you need to know will be shown to you when you need to know it. Trust your feelings, trust your visions, and all will be well."

Emmaline stood perfectly still as she listened to Susannah's words. It was all so vague, yet it seemed there was a role of amazing importance set before her. She wondered how she could do any kind of work when she did not understand what exactly she was to do or even when she was to do it. Susannah had been a friend—the very best kind of friend a little girl could have—and so Emmaline felt she had no reason to do anything except trust Susannah's words; but, trusting in something she could not understand was a tall order for Emmaline, who had always seen her world in terms of right and wrong, sensible and foolish. There were so many things she wanted to know, yet there was one question that moved to the front of her mind, which demanded to be asked. She had to know before moving forward.

"Who is the author?"

Susannah smiled.

"That is one question I cannot answer so easily. To know the author, you must begin to understand the story. They really are woven together in such a way that it is through the story that one gets to know the writer. So, learn the story, Emmaline."

"How do I do that?"

"You open up your mind, you free yourself from seeing things as always good or bad. You quit demanding that things make sense, and you believe that things you never imagined possible, could actually be possible. There is so much more to this world than you have been taught to see."

Emmaline smiled at Susannah in the small, polite way she often smiled at people when they were not making sense. It was an expression that Susannah had seen Emmaline make more than once.

And Susannah laughed softly, because she knew her friend was skeptical and that Emmaline's ability to tolerate the strange and wonderful would soon be challenged in ways the new storysmith could not imagine. Susannah tried an example. "When you see a hole in the ground, perhaps there actually is a hole in the ground, and when you do not see it anymore, perhaps it closed up before you could reach it because a storysmith somewhere fixed something that had been broken. And when you hear a voice in your head, perhaps it is your own voice, or perhaps it is a voice the writer sent to you, perhaps it is my voice guiding you to where you need to be. So many things are happening around you, if only you open your eyes and your ears and your mind to the story the writer has written, then all will be well. All will be wonderful. Remember that you are not the writer of this story, Emmaline. You are a magnificent character, but it is not you who makes the rules." And here, Susannah let out another soft little laugh and leaned close to Emmaline and whispered, "Enjoy being a character in this story, Emmaline. Your role is an amazing one."

Emmaline stood silent again, thinking about Susannah's words, thinking back to the moments earlier in the day when she had seen the hole in her front yard. *So it really had been there*, she thought to herself.

And then, as if to illustrate Susannah's point, something bright and twinkling caught the corner of Emmaline's eye. She turned toward it, blinked to adjust to the brightness of the object and then realized that what she saw—not more than an arm's reach from her face—was a beautiful hourglass, a bit smaller than her hand, but made from a brilliant, shimmering glass that produced reflections like tiny rainbows that flashed and bounced all around the glass. Even more curious, the shining hourglass in front of Emmaline's eyes was floating in space.

"It's always good to have a sense of time in a world where time is such a different thing than what you have been accustomed to. Take it," Susannah said. "It's yours. From the writer. He is a writer of gifts. All gifts don't come from him. But the really good ones do."

Emmaline took hold of the little hourglass. It was surprisingly light, yet sturdy at the same time. Emmaline saw the colored sand inside, violet and orange and gold. "It's like a little sunset inside."

"Or a sunrise," replied Susannah, "depending on how you look at it."

Emmaline slipped it into one of the pockets hidden in the folds of her crisply ironed skirt. "Thank you, or, the writer, for the gift."

"I am sure you are welcome, Emmaline. But, that brings me to a word of warning about gifts. Be cautious about accepting gifts in your adventure. If it does not help the story along to where it should go, then it is not a good gift, and it has come to you from a storychanger. Storychangers do not have any kind of creative power to compare with the writer, but sometimes, they become daring enough, dark enough, to make changes, little breaks in the story. Remember that the storychangers have no real leader. They are characters who tried to go their own way, and now they are stuck in a struggle to fit back into a story."

"Do they ever get there? Back into a story?" Emmaline asked, eager for any information she could get about this new world.

"I don't know, Emmaline. I would dearly like to know, but not all things are even for me to know. I do hope it is possible, for happy endings are the best, are they not?"

"They are."

"But this I do know: Storychangers may have tiny successes here and there, and that does make trouble and heartache and confusion for many characters along the way. And they may feel that they are on their way to changing the story to a place where they fit in again, where they can live as they hope to, yet—and this is a very important "yet"—they will never be able to replace the writer's story with their own story. Stories are written by writers, Emmaline, not by thieves. Storychangers are trying to take what someone else made and twist it, and that is something worth fighting against. Don't you think?"

"I...I do think so." And here, amidst all the seriousness of this conversation, Emmaline found her smile, and said, "You know, I have always loved stories. They matter to me."

"I do know. You will be wonderful at this work. Wonderful."

"I guess it is time to get started?"

"Yes."

"Well..."

"Goodbye," Susannah whispered. "I'll be here when you need me." And then she squeezed Emmaline's hand, urging her to be on her way.

Emmaline Hazeltree nodded, took a deep breath that moved her shoulders up a good two inches, and then gingerly placed one foot in front of the other on the smooth stone of the bridge. She was on her way.

One resolute step after the other, and Emmaline reached the other end of the bridge with no small amount of nervous fluttering in her belly. And she suddenly understood that expression—butterflies in your stomach—for that was exactly how it felt. When Emmaline had taken a few steps away from the bridge, she turned back and looked at it, the large stone passage from one mountain to the other. Susannah was still there, a far-off, blurry figure with golden hair standing out as the only distinguishable feature. Emmaline squinted, hoping to get a better view of her friend. Was Susannah waving at her or softly nodding her head, she wondered, for those gestures would have been encouraging at such a moment. Squinting did not help; the distance from one side of the bridge to the other was too great, her friend too far away. Emmaline lifted her hand, her palm held up in the air beside her and facing the direction of Susannah. She did not know whether her friend could see this movement she made, but it was the best she could do as a goodbye.

"Okay." Emmaline whispered to herself as she turned back around and looked about her. "Now what?"

She found she was no longer standing on a mountain peak. The land had transformed in the work of a moment. There was no valley before her, no water below a bridge, no mountainsides or cliff, no heights at all. There was nothing but grass, a large, open field that seemed to stretch out before her for an impossible distance. She was reminded of the simple "green" color from a new box of crayons, the one that doesn't have a complicated name, but is the shiniest and the best color of them all, the green that she would always lift out of the box first and stare at because it seemed to hold so much promise in it. She could color the best fields with that shade of green, draw the prettiest emerald jewels, the luckiest four-leaf clover. And there she found herself standing in that seemingly never-ending sea of her favorite color, and again, she felt she did not want to leave that place. She continued to have an oddly warm and comfortable feeling that made her legs feel lighter, her heart calmer. Such feeling must mean that she was exactly where she was supposed to be. For a moment Emmaline considered walking straight ahead, for there was nothing there but grass, nothing that spoke of an adventure or purpose, and she was all alone. Surely, she thought, there was no work for her to do in a place full of nothing but perfectly green grass. And then she wondered if, possibly, just maybe, she was to sit and wait in the midst of this grassy sea, for there seemed no distinct direction to travel. Perhaps someone would meet her there and tell her what to do, where to go, for why else, Emmaline Hazeltree wondered, would she feel so completely at peace, so light and content and good, if she was not exactly where she was supposed to be? She did not have much in this magical space she found herself in, but she did have her own thoughts, her own feelings, and they seemed to be telling her she was in the correct spot. And so, she let herself fall lightly down into the blades of grass, the stiff cotton skirt of her dress billowing out around her criss-crossed legs, and she skimmed her palms ever-so-gently along the top of the grass which grew all around her, and it tickled her skin.

"Yes," Emmaline said to herself, "I'll just stay here. Susannah did say to trust my feelings." And, of course, Emmaline was the kind of girl who always followed directions, so trust her feelings she would. And just as she breathed a rather loud sigh, the ring in her pocket began to sing.

Chapter Five

Watertown

Emmaline was not musically inclined. In fact, she had a rather uncooperative singing voice, and found that she lacked the ability to clap along to the beat of a song. Despite this lack of musicality, Emmaline appreciated music and could identify beautiful music when she heard it. And, as curious as having a singing ring was, it was the beauty of the sounds it made that captivated Emmaline. It was like the memory of a far away woman singing a lullaby. Emmaline, slowly and reverently, took the ring from her pocket and the music became more clear and entrancing as she looked into the ring. The voice was so lovely and sweet, and something else…it seemed to touch a distant memory. She could not quite catch the tune, but, with her musical clumsiness, she didn't really expect to. As she peered into the swirling colors of her ring, which seemed to have come alive in her hand, Emmaline became absolutely certain: She had heard this voice before.

Still unable to make out the words, for the ring's song was muffled as if it was coming from far away or was being played from an antique radio, Emmaline focused instead on trying to remember where she had heard the voice. Suddenly, Emmaline felt she should stand. It was as if her legs knew what to do while her head did not. And so she stood up in that bright green field, and she began to walk, still listening to the voice. She held the ring up to her ear, hoping that would help her recognize the voice, yet the volume seemed to stay the same to her, no matter how closely she listened. And suddenly, the ring trembled, as a person would tremble from a chill.

It was cool to the touch, and that beautiful singing became clear and low and sweeter still, until she could finally make out the final words of the song.

"Grandma's gonna sing you a lullaby."

"Grandma," Emmaline breathed out the word, feeling it being spoken for the first time in so long.

It was her grandmother's voice coming from the ring, and that made sense, which sensible Emmaline appreciated, seeing that she found herself in a very nonsensical place. The ring had belonged to her grandmother, and so, if anyone's voice would somehow be coming out of it, of course it would have been hers.

"I wonder," Emmaline's voice whispered out into the dark blue space she suddenly found herself in. The grass field had vanished just as quickly as the bridge and mountain peaks before them had gone, and now she was standing in a long and thin alley on an uneven stone street, with white laundry hanging out to dry high above her head, and open windows decorated by flower boxes and baked pies sitting on a few of the window sills to cool. She was in a city now. The sun was rising in the distance, everything around her was quiet, and somehow, without her even feeling it, her shoes had changed. Where her comfortable sneakers had been just a moment before, her feet were now laced into black leather ankle shoes, tied neatly around bright white socks. They were old-fashioned shoes, tight and thin, the sort of shoes one might expect a child to wear in a faded photograph in a history book. Nothing else on her person had changed, her yellow dress was the same, her hair still neatly pulled back from her face. Only her shoes were different, and as she headed away from the back of the narrow ally and toward the wide street ahead, she heard her steps make a *clack-clack-clack-clack* sound, which she found most disagreeable. She would certainly stick out with these shoes, she thought.

Yet, she was wrong. As she stepped out onto the street, she saw a group of little girls waiting outside of a tall, brick building. The girls had small, metal pails in hand and they were wearing shoes identical to hers. And when the thick, wooden doors on that building opened, and the girls began to move toward and up the steps and through the door, Emmaline heard the same *clack-clack-clack-clack* coming from their steps. It seemed that her strange new shoes would help her fit in here, wherever "here" was.

The little girls were all inside now, but just before the door closed, a young woman in an elegant, white, grown-up-looking dress with a large, floppy hat topped with pink flowers, slipped out the closing doors, made a huffing sound, shook her head, and stomped down the steps. Her shoes did not make such a racket, even while stomping, and so, Emmaline guessed, they must have been much daintier than her own. This young woman looked the perfect picture of a lady, Emmaline decided, despite the minor tantrum she was throwing.

Emmaline was watching this lady so intently that she was quite startled when the lady stopped squarely in front of her, narrowed her eyes at Emmaline, and struck up a conversation with her.

"You are not going into that school, I hope, are you child?"

"Um," was the most intelligent response Emmaline could manage, so stunned was she to be speaking to this woman who was obviously a great lady from another place in time.

"I sincerely hope not, child. For that school," the young lady said, pointing a gloved finger in the direction of the tall building with the wooden doors, "is no proper place for a young girl. Not one copy of a novel do they have. Not one. 'Silly books,' they call them. Silly! And here I wanted to make a donation of a shelf full of novels to their library! Can you imagine such a school, believing novels silly?"

Emmaline blinked, gulped, and then somehow found the presence of mind to nod.

"You can imagine?" the lady asked. "You *can*? How dreadful then, that a young mind such as yours can fathom such a dreary notion." The lady sighed, straightening a large pin protruding from her larger hat. "Let me tell you this, and you shall owe me no thanks for this bit of wisdom, as I offer it freely to a beauty of a girl such as yourself: Novels are treasures. Their inclusion in a school library is as justified as field journals of the natural sciences and volumes on mathematics. A novel can take you places, as I hope you are aware."

So can rings, Emmaline thought, sighing and looking down at the ring.

The young woman's glance followed Emmaline's down to the hand that was holding the ring between two tightly squeezing fingers. The lady gasped, "Oh, this ring! How astonishing! This ring looks so like my mother's ring. I had thought it the most beautiful ring in the world, but now I see it has a match for beauty! Where ever did you get such a ring?"

"It, it was my grandma's." Emmaline was thankful she could answer the lady's question truthfully and believably at the same time.

"I see." The lady paused, looking at Emmaline with a half smile. "And what is your name, and what errand are you off to with this valuable ring at such an early hour in the morning?"

Emmaline's head spun with possible answers. She could say that she was on her way to the jeweler to have it cleaned, or that she had put the ring on while playing pretend and then accidentally left the house with it still on her finger. But then, Emmaline decided, she would stick with the truth. Because if she really was doing some sort of important work, if her being a storysmith really was a good thing, then she did not want to soil it with lies.

And so, Emmaline said simply, "I'm just doing as I was told."

"Oh, of course you are," the lady smiled a pretty and full smile. "Of course you are my dear. And what, may I ask, is your name? I am Gwendolyn Waters."

"Emmaline Hazeltree."

And here, Emmaline decided to take a chance, to speak a further truth with this Gwendolyn Waters. So far, in her short time as a storysmith, Emmaline had discovered that all she needed to do was to trust her feelings, and she would continue to make progress on her journey, just as Susannah had said. And the glad feeling Emmaline got when she saw Gwendolyn's smile made the girl feel as though this person could be trusted.

And so, Emmaline admitted to Gwendolyn Waters, "I don't know where I am or where I'm supposed to be."

Gwendolyn bent down a little, getting closer to Emmaline's eye level and spoke with such confidence that Emmaline decided she had been right to confide in her.

"I shall help you find your way, Emmaline. Now, let's see. What is it your grandmother sent you to do? Something with the ring, a jeweler maybe? Perhaps that is a good place to begin, you explaining your errand to me."

"Maybe first you could tell me where we are."

"Ah, yes, very wise, Emmaline." Gwendolyn swept her arm out to her side, gesturing to the thoroughfare they were standing on. "This is East Main Street, where the Watertown Centennial Founders Day Celebration will take place tomorrow. If you have an errand to complete here, then I suggest we hurry to it, as this thoroughfare will soon become even more crowded with preparations. My, there are booths and carts already setting up. It's even busier than last year."

The Watertown Centennial Founders Day Celebration...Emmaline knew this event. She had heard this story so many times, when she was younger, from her grandfather, before her grandmother had fallen ill and taken to a life of bed rest in the farmhouse, back when he would tell stories and smile often. Her great-grandparents had met and fallen in love all in one day, in their town of Watertown, a town named for her great-grandmother's family. And this meeting had taken place, she had heard her grandma tell her time and time again, as the town was preparing for the Watertown Centennial Founders Day Celebration. There had been street vendors and decorations and a fireworks show full of red and blue flashes in the sky. She could hear her grandfather's voice now, repeating the story over in her head, "My mother, Gwen," her grandfather had always begun the story, "was a fine and beautiful lady." Emmaline had forgotten until that moment that her grandfather, the tall and serious man of the farmhouse, had once been a great storyteller. Time, it seemed to Emmaline, had changed him. And now, Emmaline knew, as she stood in front of Gwendolyn Waters, "in the year of 19 and 11," (her grandfather always cited the year and said it just so), that her grandfather had not been embellishing the tale. Her great-grandmother truly was a fine and beautiful lady. Also, she was a helpful one, for it seemed she would help Emmaline, the storysmith, find her way.

Chapter Six

Resting

It might be assumed that coming face to face with her great-grandmother, who had passed away decades ago, but who was now as alive as could be and offering to help Emmaline in a moment when she needed it, would be a great comfort to Emmaline in her extraordinary situation. However, this was not the case. No,

Emmaline did not feel comfortable or safe, or even excited. This is the moment in her story when Emmaline, quite frankly, snapped. Emmaline's willingness to accept what she did not understand had a limit. Having this conversation with Gwendolyn Waters, who was very much alive and a young lady, no less, but who was also Emmaline's long-deceased great-grandmother, well, that surpassed the limit.

"This is crazy."

"Pardon me, Emmaline."

Emmaline suddenly needed to sit. She crumpled down onto criss-crossed legs, her elbows plopping down onto her knees, and her chin smacking down on her palms.

"Is this real? I mean, really real? I was fine with the movies of my life, fine with Susannah and the bridge, and somehow I was okay with the ring singing to me, but you, you are my limit."

Gwendolyn was kneeling down beside her, brows knitting together, her hand reaching out to touch Emmaline's forehead, checking for a fever.

"Child, child. Calm yourself. You are much too warm. Come," Gwendolyn said, tugging at Emmaline's arm and bringing her back to her feet. "You shall have a rest."

****

Gwendolyn Waters lived in the finest house Emmaline had ever seen. It was tall, stately, and painted white, with a porch on each floor that wrapped around the front and along one side of the house. And now Emmaline was being led inside its ink-blue front door.

"Now," Gwendolyn said, pulling two giant pins from her hat and handing them along with the hat to a woman in a black dress and white apron. "You shall rest. No more of this silly ranting. Conversation is an art, young lady, and when we are overtired and overwrought, the art falls away, and it is at this moment that nonsense may work its useless self into our conversations. So, you shall go upstairs, third door on the right, Amelia will lead you there." Gwendolyn nodded in the direction of the maid, who looked kind, yet seemed to be studying Emmaline's hair, as though regarding its simple, albeit tousled, style as a curiousity. "You shall lie down, rest, and do not get up again until your sense has returned." Here, Gwendolyn paused her speech and looked down at her great-granddaughter, without, of course, any inkling that it was in fact her great-granddaughter, and, as if she had suddenly thought of something important that she had forgotten, asked "You do have sense, do you not, Emmaline? I have not judged incorrectly, have I?"

Emmaline's mouth opened, her mind searching for words to relay her distress, to explain to her everything she had experienced and seen that day, to tell her everything she was afraid of, unsure of, everything she was confused about and all the times and people and paths and emotions she had taken in today; her parents splitting up, her grandfather waiting at the supper table, her best friend being some supernatural advisor, and now, her deceased great-grandmother alive and young and standing in front of her in the past. And as her mouth held open, all these words did not come. There were so many things she did not understand, so many things she was taking in. She felt like she knew nothing. She was a storysmith, but what was that exactly? She did not even know. She only had a broad explanation from Susannah, but no real details, no exact instructions. And so, Emmaline Hazeltree answered her great-grandmother's question, telling her the only thing she felt she knew to be true in that moment, the only words that would come to her.

"Yes, I have sense. I just can't make any right now."

"Oh, dear girl!" Gwendolyn laughed. "That is exactly how one should feel in this world from time to time. That is exactly the way of things. Now, you rest, and no more of this falling to the ground and talk of reaching your limits. For I assure you, there are a great many limits left for you to meet and surpass in this life. I have a good feeling about you. Now, off for a nap and then we shall help you with your errand. Do take care with that ring now, Emmaline. It is quite precious, I'm sure."

Emmaline felt odd inside. Her head felt heavy and unsteady. Her feet were tired and her heels were sore, probably more from the shoes than from the walk across the bridge earlier that day. Her eyes stung with the tears she had been holding back since the morning car ride with her parents when they had announced they were breaking up or whatever it was they were considering. With all of this magic and newness around her, she still felt the pain deep in her heart. For a child's family is never too far away from her. As Emmaline stood in the quiet of the Waters' guest room, she felt that going through both of these stories—the one back with her family and the story unfolding here in the past—was just too much, that she had truly reached her limit. Her moment of anxiety, of falling down on the sidewalk and proclaiming that she could take no more, was not an act. This single day had been more eventful than her entire last year had been—than her entire life had been, really. She shivered as she untied the thin laces of her shoes, removed them, and set them neatly at the foot of the bed. She decided maybe she did need a rest. And she did not know what else to do, so maybe a nap really was the best thing for her. She grasped a carved, wooden post that extended from the bed frame up toward the ceiling and hopped up onto the tall bed with too many pillows, and she sank down into the nest of quilt and mattress that rose up around her, and she closed her eyes.

She was alone now, in this huge house, back in time, and yet, she knew that somehow she would be led to exactly where she needed to be. She took the ring out of her pocket and placed it on her thumb where it fit snugly. She felt a warmth creep through her toes, and her shivering subsided. She believed all would be well. Not because the ring was magic, but because it was with her. Emmaline only needed to remember the ring, to feel its smooth band, to see the internal glow of its stone, to understand that she was in the right place. Suddenly she was glad to be where she was. She relaxed into a giant pillow and pulled the thick cloth of the quilt around her. She drifted off to sleep, her right hand holding on to her left thumb where she wore the ring.

****

Emmaline saw Susannah and thought that she must be dreaming, and she was correct about that, yet, this was no ordinary dream. This was the dream of a storysmith at work.

"Where are we?"

"I'm in the Place of Stillness, where you left me, Emmaline." Susannah's voice was soft and steady, as though she were a teacher instructing a young pupil. "While you are in a guest room in the home of the Waters family, many years before you began your journey this morning."

"I don't understand."

"Yes, yes, that is perfectly natural." Susannah breathed out a little sigh, the kind one emits when humor and annoyance and patience all mingle together in a confused way. "I have told the fact checkers time and again that a manual on storysmithing would be the best thing for those like you. It does seem like it is rather a lot to take in all at once. One moment you are a normal girl living your life in your time, moving along steadily, and then the next, you are weaving in and out of decades and up and down the globe, ensuring the story all falls into place properly."

"Falls into place properly?" Emmaline's eyes widened, her hand reached out and grabbed onto Susannah's hand, which felt perfectly real despite being a dream. "But what needs to fall into place properly? What am I to do?"

"To be a good storysmith, you have to be a good reader of the story. Watch as the story unfolds. Listen to your feelings when you encounter its characters. Believe who you feel is trustworthy, and no one else. Pay special attention to the small details; while some people gloss over them, a good storysmith gathers up the insights provided by small things. And, most importantly, don't fret, Emmaline. Trust that there is a story taking place, even when things don't make sense. You are with Gwendolyn Waters now, so see where she leads you. I cannot tell you exactly what to do, because I do not know. But I cannot wait to find out. This is the exciting part. You are finally here, Emmaline. I truly have been waiting so long for this. You're here!" Susannah's hands clapped together as a smile spread across her face, and Emmaline remembered Susannah clapping when she counted two hundred jumps with her new jump rope that Emmaline spun for her, the other end wedged in the crook of a tree. Susannah was thrilled to be in this moment, Emmaline could see that all over her face, the bright eyes, the dimples framing her big smile. Emmaline wished she could feel that same excitement. Perhaps, she wondered, that would come later. She hoped so.

"Why couldn't you tell me this before? Why wouldn't you tell me to find Gwendolyn and let her lead me around, or at least warn me about running into my great-grandmother on the street?"

"Everything has a time, Emmaline. If you knew everything there was to know at once, then your responsibility would be much too great, your danger far too deep, your adventure far too impossible. It is all perfectly placed this way. Do not worry. Rest in the knowledge that you will have exactly the wisdom, exactly the path, that you need when you need it. Like a candle to light your way. And I'm here to help you with that. That's my part in this work. When you need direction, simply ask, and help will come. Just remember that help may not look like what you expect. Help comes in many forms. And while you rest, whether in a nap or just as you take a few moments to catch your breath or pause in your adventure, I'll help you find your way. It is all very simple, really."

"I don't see how any of this is simple."

"Not yet, you don't. But you will. When you allow your mind to let loose of all the worry, to let the walls come down, and you open up to a new understanding of things, you'll find this: The things you once thought complicated or even impossible, may actually be the simplest and truest things of all. Now, rest, Emmaline. You now know what a storysmith does.

When you wake, look out for things around you that don't seem quite right, that don't fit with the story as you know it. It's your role to ensure things happen as they should."

"Is there anything else you can tell me?"

"For now, there is only one thing more. Be aware of those who would ruin the plan. Remember, as I told you before, where there are storysmiths, there are also storychangers, those who seek to make the story their own, and while they stand no real chance of taking things over, they must not be successful in making minor shifts in the story here or there, for even that could be tragic."

"What do these storychangers look like?" Emmaline's voice was urgent now, for she felt the dream world fading, felt her toes wiggling under the heavy quilt as she began to wake up.

"Like anyone else. It's their hearts that are different."

Emmaline pulled the quilt up higher around her neck as she left the dream world. She knew the dream world had been real. There could be no questioning it, for in her hand, there was a blue ribbon, just like the ribbons that had been tied to the end of Susannah's braids. She wasn't sure if this proof of the dream's reality was comforting or frightening. And she wondered, for the first time, if maybe it was possible to be both comforted and frightened at the same time. The world was turning out to be a much more complex place than Emmaline had ever found it to be before this summer, and the summer was just beginning— both of them. For, it seemed, there were two summers happening for Emmaline at the same time. There was the summer happening back at the farmhouse with her grandfather, the one in which she was broken-hearted and lonely. And then there was this summer, the one that had really happened long, long ago; yet, here she was, experiencing it, as well. It was all so strange, but Emmaline believed she was there for a reason. She only needed to figure out what in this world that reason was.

Chapter Seven

A Little Ridiculousness

Emmaline laced up her new shoes, still not at all pleased with their stiffness. It really was a bother to wear uncomfortable shoes, but these would just have to do, since her others had vanished when these polished, antique-looking shoes had appeared on her feet. She loved the look of them, but the lack of comfort was disappointing and not worth their classic aesthetic. She wiggled her toes, holding her legs out in front of her from her perch on the edge of the bed. A hard, squeezing sound came from the new leather of the shoes as they tried to bend along with her movement.

"Time to get moving, I suppose," she whispered to herself. It seemed she was getting quite used to talking to herself. For in this time and place, she really was the only person with whom she was truly able to speak about such things when Susannah was not around.

What would her great-grandmother think if she marched down the stairs, went right up to her, and proclaimed, "I am your great-granddaughter, from the future, of course. And I absolutely cannot stand these unyielding shoes. Also, congratulations on your future happiness! You are to meet your husband today!" That probably would not go over so well, she decided. So, for now, she would continue to confide in herself.

Just as Emmaline jumped off the bed and smoothed down her hair and straightened her skirt and sweater, there was a soft knock on the door.

"Come in?" Emmaline thought her voice sounded more like a question than an invitation. She cleared her throat, hoping some confidence would come to her.

"Well," Gwendolyn almost sang, as she stepped into the room, "and how are you feeling now? Much improved, I do hope. I do always say that a rest is the best thing when one seems to have lost her bearings. Do you not agree? Do you not feel much improved?"

"Yes, I do agree. I am, I mean. Much improved." Emmaline found herself staring at her silly, black shoes wishing she knew what to say, what she was to do in this place, for she feared that until a little more clarity came to her about what to do next, she would be nothing but a disappointment to her great-grandmother, or Gwendolyn, as it seemed more appropriate to call her.

"Excellent. Now, shall we be off?" Gwendolyn moved to stand in front of the large gilt-framed mirror in the center of the room, where she brushed back a few strands of sun-colored hair from her forehead, tucking it into the elaborate hairstyle that swept away from her kindly face.

"Okay," Emmaline's voice now sounded rather like a toad, and so she attempted to clear her throat again, this time hoping for more success in reclaiming her regular, clear voice. "Let's get going then."

There, that sounded better, Emmaline thought. *I can do thi*s.

"Right," Gwendolyn nodded, and then she briskly walked past Emmaline, who then followed her down the grand staircase, her hand sliding down the polished banister, her eyes watching the red-carpeted stairs as she carefully stepped down them.

"Now," Gwendolyn said, "I've taken the liberty of fetching one of my old hats for you. It isn't so fretfully out of style. I am not so ancient that the fashions have changed a great deal since my girlhood, you know. I noticed you must have misplaced your hat, and so this shall be yours for the day. Or you may keep it, of course, if you fancy it."

It was a sweet little hat, Emmaline thought, woven of soft straw with a midnight blue silk ribbon tied snugly around the base of the crown.

"Thank you."

"You're quite welcome, of course." And in that moment, Emmaline thought she saw a change in Gwendolyn. She had softened a bit when she received the thanks from Emmaline. Up until that moment, her tone had been authoritative, not rude, but a little guarded, and her expression had been like a mask of confidence and importance. Yet, now, she looked much softer, almost wistful, like something new was happening to her, and she didn't quite know what. Emmaline smiled as she felt the presence of the ring on her thumb, and she closed her fingers around it. She closed her eyes and listened, thinking that perhaps this shift in demeanor had been a sign of some sort.

And Emmaline, it seemed, was correct. As her fingertips clasped the ring on her thumb, she heard two things simultaneously. There was a sharp set of knocks coming from the front door of the Waters house. And, there was the twinkling sound of bells, sounding at precisely the same rhythm as the knocks. Their sound was bright and clear and almost magical, and they seemed to come from somewhere in the distance.

Startled by these striking noises, Emmaline's hand loosened its grasp on the ring, and when the door knocker sounded again, there were no more bells twinkling strong and clear in the distance. The magic had gone, but the message had been made clear: This knock on the door meant something important.

And then, as if Gwendolyn had read Emmaline's thoughts, she looked down at Emmaline, while pulling on her bright white gloves, and said, "Oh, that's nothing important, Emmaline. Simply someone delivering a parcel to my father, I'm sure. We will leave the door for Amelia to tend to, and we shall be off by way of the side door quickly and easily. Nothing will detain us here when we have a mission to be on, dear girl!"

"Wait!" Emmaline cried out, her voice loud and trembling, as if her very life depended on it (and perhaps it did, considering she really had no idea what would happen if she failed to help the story go as planned).

"Heavens! Whatever is the matter?" Gwendolyn's hand flew to her chest, as though the shock of Emmaline's words had caused her heart to leap forward.

"It's just that…" And here Emmaline Hazeltree made a decision about her work as a storysmith, one which would remain with her throughout this journey and all the journeys that followed. Before she spoke, hoping to convince Gwendolyn not to ignore whatever or whomever was behind that front door, Emmaline decided she would not lie as she went about her work. Being the sensible girl she was born to be, she understood that she was tasked with an important mission, and lying would only taint her work and soil her part in the story, and that is not something she wished for. She wanted to be good, and goodness has a hard time shining through in the muck of lies. Susannah had once told her this over a game of checkers one summer day, and she had never forgotten it.

And so, instead of making up some silly tale to get Gwendolyn to answer the door herself, Emmaline says, simply and honestly, "I don't know why, but I think the maid shouldn't answer the door this time. I think you should."

Gwendolyn looked at Emmaline, the lady's face changing slowly from confusion to happy amusement. One side of her mouth quirked up a bit, her eyes narrowed and brightened at the same time. She nodded once, quickly, down at Emmaline, and then, Gwendolyn reached out her gloved hand, pulled open the heavy front door, and, smiling, she greeted the young man who had been knocking: a stranger with light, red hair and the greenest eyes Emmaline had ever seen, that is, on anyone other than her father. This had to be her great-grandfather, Jonah Hazeltree. And he was looking down at Gwendolyn with a similar expression to the one Gwendolyn had worn only a moment before; he was amused, and happily so, with the young woman standing before him. Amused so much it seemed, that he couldn't help but laugh.

And while this does seem like a promising beginning for the soon-to-be happy couple (for what is a better sign than a smile and laughter?), it was not to be so simple, for, it seems, Gwendolyn was not exactly the kind of girl one might call "sensible," at least not so sensible as her great-granddaughter, Emmaline. No, Gwendolyn Waters was the type of girl who was ruled by her emotions first and foremost, and it rapidly grew apparent to Emmaline that Gwendolyn's emotions had been upset suddenly and dangerously by Jonah

Hazeltree. Gwendolyn Waters, this visitor would soon learn, did not like to be laughed at. Not at all. Especially by a complete stranger who looked at her as if she were some sort of circus attraction.

"What can be the meaning of such rude manners?" The low fierceness in Gwendolyn's voice was enough to halt Jonah's laughter, yet not enough to wipe the smile clear from his face. No, he would not be deterred from whatever had amused him.

"Forgive me, Miss. It's just that the world is such a splendid place today, don't you think?"

Gwendolyn's eyes narrowed as she responded, "I do not catch your meaning." Her hand held onto the doorknob, preparing, it appeared, to close it soundly, as Jonah continued to stand there smiling.

"Oh, now do not fault me a little poor manners, a little joy on such a day as this. I am just here to deliver a map to Mister LeGrand Waters, as it has just been completed for him. You see, I'm newly arrived on your continent. This is my first day in this country, and here I have work with a mapmaker, a sun shining above, a celebration setting up in town, and then I am sent to the finest house in Watertown, and who opens the door for the likes of me, but the Lady of the house herself! A Lady opening the door for me? It is quite a wonderful day, can you not see?"

Emmaline's gaze moved back and forth, back and forth, from her great-grandfather to her great-grandmother. She found his little speech quite nice and hoped that Gwendolyn did, as well, but her great-grandmother simply stood there, silent and still, as the seconds moved by, her hand still clutching the door knob.

No, this silence could not be a good thing, Emmaline thought, for up until that moment, Gwendolyn Waters had been talkative and assertive, not in the least bit quiet or passive. So Emmaline decided she must intervene. These two people before her must get along, *they must*. She wondered suddenly if perhaps this was her task: to make sure these two would meet and get along that day. She knew she must make sure everything went according to plan, according to the story, the way it should. But this could be difficult, to be a child in the room with two near grown-ups, and to be the one to take control of the situation. Emmaline believed that adults didn't often listen to children, not really, not when emotions were flying and adults were laughing or cross or were busy making up their own minds about something. But she must intervene. She simply must. She was a storysmith, for goodness' sake, so she took one small step forward and gently placed her hand on top of Gwendolyn's where it gripped the door knob, and she guided the door open just a small bit more.

Well, this movement did two things: It caused Jonah to pull his gaze away from Gwendolyn's face and nod a polite greeting in his great-granddaughter's direction, and it caused Gwendolyn to snap out of her silence, clear her throat in an almost-lady-like fashion, and then to proclaim, "I am not the Lady of the house. I am her daughter."

She reached for the leather portfolio in Jonah's hand, and he handed it to her as he continued to smile. She nodded, rather brusquely, and then closed the door. Gwendolyn's free hand reached for her heart, Emmaline noticed, as if she felt the need to steady herself. *Odd*, Emmaline thought.

And then Gwendolyn looked down at Emmaline, her eyes wide, her head tilted a bit to the side and asked, "Now why in the world did I say that?"

Emmaline tread carefully, so as not to upset the story pieces any more than they may have already been upset by her interfering, for it really was a difficult thing to make a story work when you were right in the middle of it and had no time to pause and evaluate things before proceeding. "Why did you say what?"

"Any of it. All of it, I suppose. Heavens, about his manners, and the part about my being the daughter and not the Lady. Who is he that I explain my situation to him? How very..."

"Surprising?" Emmaline offered, before any negative adjective could come out of Gwendolyn's mouth, because she really didn't want any negative thoughts swirling around if these two were to get along happily.

"I was going to say 'ridiculous.'"

Emmaline giggled then. Because that really was the perfect word, and she just couldn't help herself. This whole situation was absolutely ridiculous. A little girl making sure her great-grandparents had a pleasant first meeting, or at least, not a disastrous one. Ridiculous indeed. The sudden giggling coming from Emmaline, who had been all seriousness in front of Gwendolyn up until that point, caused Gwendolyn to laugh a little at herself, just a small, soft, and very short-lived laugh. Yet, laughter it was. And Emmaline was glad of it. "'Ridiculous' is the better word, I think."

"Absolutely." Gwendolyn nodded, her air of confidence and certainty seeming to return after her brief moments of discomposure in the presence of Jonah Hazeltree. "Ridiculous indeed."

"You know, Gwendolyn, sometimes a little ridiculousness is just what a person needs. Don't you think?" Not waiting for a response, Emmaline stepped past her great-grandmother, through the doorway and outside, smiling both in spite of and because of the whole situation.

Chapter Eight

Lemon Ices

Just when Emmaline had found some humor in the day, as she laughed at the ridiculousness of it all, while her shoes made sharp clicking sounds as she stepped down from the stone steps outside the entrance to the Waters house and onto the brick sidewalk, a memory flew to the front of her mind. A lemon ice. A lemon ice! When she had heard the romantic tale of her great-grandfather and great-grandmother meeting and falling in love all in one day, the story had always included the sweet, little detail that, within moments of meeting, Jonah Hazeltree had treated Miss Gwendolyn Waters to a lemon ice from a cart on the street. *Within moments of meeting!* These words rang out in Emmaline's head loudly and over and over until she felt dizzy and panicked. A slight buzzing began in her ears amid the phrase *"moments of meeting!"* being repeated again and again in her mind. She had to do something, but she didn't know what or how. The story could not change. She had to make sure things fell into place properly, and just when she felt overcome, lost and utterly useless, she saw it: a metal cart being pushed down the street on two large, wooden wheels by a short gentleman, who was shaped rather like the cart wheels and who was wearing an oversized straw hat. And then Emmaline heard the man shout, "Lemon ices! Lemon ices! There's nothing sweeter to celebrate the founding of Watertown than a nice, cold, lemon ice!"

So there was the lemon ice cart, and, of course, Gwendolyn was walking right beside her, but where was Jonah? *Surely he could not have gone far*, she thought, for he had just been at the Waters' front door only moments before. And then she saw him, one block straight ahead, but he was stopped on the sidewalk and had turned to look at something. It was difficult to see details at such a distance, but Emmaline thought he was looking back at them, or perhaps down at the lemon ice cart, his hand held to his brow, probably to block out the sun to better get a look. Oh, wouldn't that have made this part of the story fall into place so well! Emmaline's racing heart slowed down, she smoothed her trembling hands down her wrinkled, yellow skirt to help continue to calm herself, for matters really seemed to be working out so well. Perhaps she wouldn't need to intervene in this part of the story at all, which was a relief to Emmaline, as the uncertainty of her duties was still heavy on her mind.

It seemed as though Gwendolyn and Jonah were both going to be moving in the direction of the lemon ice cart, as Jonah had indeed started walking again. So there they were: all headed toward the lemon ice cart, and surely, surely, Jonah would purchase a lemon ice for Gwendolyn, and perhaps that would make her forget about the awkward or rude or ridiculous moment in the entranceway of her house, and then she would fall in love with him, and then they would head straight away to get married, and then Emmaline's work as a storysmith would be accomplished. If, of course, this was even her job, which, of course, she was merely guessing at in that moment.

Before they could reach the wooden-wheeled cart and the man with the straw hat, something else happened, or rather, someone happened. A young man, just about the age of Gwendolyn, and judging by his smooth brown hat and his shining shoes, also of the same social class as Gwendolyn (which really did matter a great deal to many people in that time), appeared from across the street. He stepped right up to the cart, fanned out some paper money, and purchased lemon ices. Two of them.

As Emmaline and Gwendolyn approached the cart, the young man with the shining shoes extended one of his hands, with a small glass of the frozen lemon treat in it, toward Gwendolyn, and he said, "For you, Miss Waters."

Emmaline felt as though a heavy stone had sunk to the bottom of her stomach and landed with a *thud*. This was not how the story was supposed to go. And now there stood Jonah, who had just reached the lemon ice cart, hands in his pockets, looking rather hopeless, and then, something delightful happened, he winked at Emmaline. Emmaline suddenly cheered, having her great-grandfather wink at her. This sweet, little connection boosted her spirits. Emmaline believed in her great-grandfather, even though he hadn't heard this story before, she had a feeling that he had matters under control. But, how would he get Gwendolyn to accept a lemon ice from him, when she already had one?

"Why thank you, Mr. Daniels. Such a lovely gesture."

This young man, whose hair glistened with some sort of oily hair product, smiled a dreadfully smarmy smile at Gwendolyn and said, "Lovely gestures are a gentleman's greatest purpose, I would say." And, turning to Jonah, whom Mr. Daniels did not seem to acknowledge as an equal, he said, "Don't you agree, sir?" Mr. Daniels continued to smile, but his head tilted slightly to the side, like a little bird, with the slightest hint of mockery. And then Mr. Daniels strode off, without so much as a nod, or bow, or words of parting to Miss Waters, who stood there, lemon ice in hand.

And then, Gwendolyn turned to Emmaline, held out the lemon ice and said, "You must enjoy this for me. Treats are best meant for children, are they not?" Emmaline took the lemon ice. Feeling the frosty glass as her fingers wrapped around it, she saw Jonah hold up two fingers and kindly order two lemon ices from the man in the straw hat. And then Gwendolyn Waters was handed a lemon ice in a cool glass cup from a gentleman for the second time in the space of a moment. But, this time, this lemon ice, had been purchased by Jonah Hazeltree. The story had been righted. Somehow.

"I'd say treats are for everyone."

"Oh, I couldn't possibly accept…" Gwendolyn started to say.

"Don't go letting a young man's well-earned-and-spent wage melt right in front of his eyes, please

Miss. That would be a heart-breaking thing to do. I know ladies aren't always the easiest on a man trying to impress, but please don't tell me you are that pitiless."

Emmaline looked up at Gwendolyn who was clearly giving Jonah's words thought before she responded. Moments passed without a word, and then, Emmaline, sensing that Gwendolyn wasn't quite sure she knew what she wanted to do, took a bite of her own tart lemon ice, and said to Gwendolyn, "It really is delicious. Don't let it go to waste."

Gwendolyn sighed, and then lifted her chin just slightly and said in that proud manner Emmaline was growing accustomed to, "This does in no way undo your lazy manners from earlier; however, for the child's sake," and here, Gwendolyn inclined her head down at Emmaline, the soft feather in her hat swaying a bit with the movement, "I shall accept your kindness. But, mostly, to preserve this lovely moment for my young friend. She is a sensitive sort, I do believe." And then, Gwendolyn sighed again, this one even more exaggerated than the first, and continued, "And perhaps you are, as well. Thank you for your thoughtfulness."

Jonah Hazeltree's eyes twinkled, and his lips tightened together as if holding back a grin with great effort. He nodded and then reached for his own lemon ice from the vendor.

And then Emmaline Hazeltree enjoyed a tart, frozen lemon ice with her two great-grandparents, which really wouldn't have been such a terribly extraordinary thing, for children are often taken out for ice cream or sweet treats by grandparents; yet, this time, on this occasion, it was extraordinary; and only Emmaline knew they were a family, or at least, they would be, hopefully, if all went according to the story.

Chapter Nine

Rings and Pointed Fingers

Although Gwendolyn Waters was the sort of person to be ruled by her emotions, she did not usually allow her emotions to deviate her from following social protocol. As soon as their lemon ices were finished, she insisted that she and Emmaline move on. "We cannot remain on the sidewalk with a young man unchaperoned for more than a moment or two. And besides, what in the world would we three have in common to discuss?" And she laughed as they walked away.

Emmaline laughed, too, for she felt that Gwendolyn would soon be proven wrong. And just as she had this thought, Jonah suddenly caught up with them and politely asked if he might see Miss Waters at the fireworks display that night. Emmaline, and quite possibly Gwendolyn, smiled, nodded a goodbye at Jonah, and continued walking along.

As they walked, Emmaline took in the scene around her, noticing the details much more closely than she had before. The Founders Day Celebration in Watertown was basically a fair, her grandfather had explained to her, and even decades in the past, a fair was a familiar thing to Emmaline. She breathed in the scent of roasted corn and smoked meat, took in the sights of multi-colored banners. People smiled as they moved slowly down the street, taking everything in— the street vendors' carts, the gazebo in the town square decorated with roses and white cotton streamers, the wagons full of watermelons waiting to be cut and shared. Emmaline had always found the day before a fair to be even more exciting than the fair itself. Preparation, expectation, and possibility sparked through the air on the day before a fair. Everyone was getting ready, everyone hoping for the best. Of course, a story-loving girl like Emmaline would love a day like this. It was such a wonderful scene for a story's beginning. She found herself smiling, thinking of herself as a character in a story, within such a hopeful scene.

Now, Emmaline thought, *I'll just have to keep my eye out for Jonah as the day goes on. The more meetings these two have the better. Perhaps my job here is to help their own little fairy tale play out, almost like a young fairy godmother, but instead of helping Cinderella on her way to the ball, I am to help Gwendolyn on her way to finding Jonah.* Emmaline decided she liked the idea of herself as a fairy godmother, or more fittingly, as a fairy great-granddaughter.

As this fine sense of purpose was welling up within Emmaline, Gwendolyn led them toward the local jewelry shop to have Emmaline's ring cleaned, which had been Gwendolyn's suggestion. According to her, the ring was quite in need of a cleaning and the young lady had guessed that perhaps this was the errand Emmaline had been sent on. Emmaline, having no better idea where to go and what to do next, readily agreed to visit the jewelry shop. But as the pair walked down the bustling, pre-fair streets of Watertown, a curious, uncomfortable feeling overcame Emmaline's pleasant thoughts of being a fairy great-granddaughter. She felt uncertain about the idea that her role here was as secondary as simply hanging around as her great-grandparents fell in love. Could it be so simple? Would her purpose slip by while she enjoyed a lemon ice and strolled down the streets of Watertown? *Trying to follow all these feelings and thoughts around is exhausting,* Emmaline grumbled to herself. *And I'm the one to make sure the story works? If only I had an instruction manual or a map.* A strange place with an important job and no specific instructions made for a confusing situation to sensible Emmaline. But it was all she had at the moment, so she just took a deep breath and walked along with her great-grandmother, hoping the correct next step would present itself.

Emmaline looked down at the ring which had turned a much deeper shade of blue. It almost looked indigo, and the gem seemed to be made up of swirling waves, rather than of a solid piece of mineral. Just as Emmaline held it nearer to her face to get a better look at it, she and Gwendolyn stepped into the jewelry shop.

This was not like the jewelry stores in the mall back home where Emmaline had looked at birth stone sets under glass counters. No, this jewelry shop was more like a museum, a beautiful museum with polished wood cases with sparkling, glass panels enclosing the displays of fine old necklaces, and silver trays with detailed etchings, and opened pocket watches of gold, ticking away the seconds of this important day. There was carpet of deep red, which silenced her clicking shoes, and there were beautiful lamps made of green and purple glass, giving the shop a glow that seemed the perfect setting for one of Emmaline's mystery books.

Gwendolyn's gloved fingertips delicately tapped on the shining golden bell on the central counter, and a man in a black suit with a bright silver pocket watch in his hand, which was attached to a chain fastened to his striped black vest, walked up to the counter. He clicked the watch shut, raised his brows high and smiled as he looked at Gwendolyn.

"Miss Waters."

"Mr. Tally."

He smiled then, a look of genuine happiness lighting his face, as his shoulders raised a little higher, as if Gwendolyn's knowing his name or speaking it made him a bit proud. Emmaline realized that, of course, this would be the case, for the Waters family was considered the most important family in town. This really was a strange time and world to live in, Emmaline thought, when family history and money determined the way people treated you. Looking up at Gwendolyn, Emmaline decided that while this might seem a fine thing for one in her position, it must have also been tiresome, and even sad, to be known or unknown, to be respected or disrespected, simply for the family one was born into, rather than for one's own merits and personality.

"How may I be of assistance?"

"I've brought a friend with me today. This is Miss Emmaline. Miss Emmaline, this is Mr. Tally. Miss Emmaline has brought along her grandmother's ring for cleaning. It seems her grandmother is of like mind with my own mother, for you know, she trusts no one to clean her jewels but a jeweler. So, here we are."

Mr. Tally smiled, a small smile, for he did not appear to be the type to flash big cheeky grins or to let a wholehearted smile take over his expression. And as he held out his hand and rather politely asked, "May I?," to Emmaline and waited for her to place the ring in his hand, Emmaline smiled back.

It was all a very pleasant encounter with small smiles all around, until Mr. Tally's eyes widened, he cleared his throat, and then closed his fingers around the ring Emmaline had only just placed in his hand. His small smile straightened to a tight line, which let the following icy words issue forth: *This ring was stolen.*

Emmaline felt sick. She felt as if her heart dropped down into her stomach, and her mind felt full of swirls. Gwendolyn reached out and held onto Emmaline's hand, while Mr. Tally reached out and grabbed her by her other arm.

"This girl is no friend of yours, I assure you, Miss Waters. This girl is a thief. She has fooled you, and

I daresay you will do well not to be so trusting in the future."

"Unhand this child immediately, Mr. Tally! She is a child, not a thief."

"I assure you, Miss Waters, she is both. This ring is a Waters family jewel, and I should know. I designed and crafted it with my own hands for none other than your mother. She has tricked you, Miss Waters. I do not know what story she has told you and, of course, I shall assume that you are innocent in this and would never remove your mother's ring from her residence without her permission. How clever of this little thief to befriend you for the purpose of acquiring such a prized possession, for who would ever suspect a young girl of such a crime? Very deceptive, no?"

The way he said "no," with a lightness to his menacing voice, his chin titled slightly toward Emmaline, awaiting her response, sent a warning to Emmaline's mind. She narrowed her eyes and focused her gaze on this man who accused her of thievery, trying not to shrink from the accusation and striving to stay aware of her surroundings as a storysmith should.

"No," Emmaline said.

From between his teeth, Mr. Tally hissed out a little laugh, a small and sinister sound, dismissing Emmaline's response.

"Mr. Tally, you are speaking out of turn in countless ways. Seeing that the ring you are speaking of belongs to my family, and certainly not to yours, you will unhand it. You will unhand this girl, and you will apologize." Gwendolyn's cheeks were red, her chin tilted down and to the side, the feather in her hat bouncing as she spoke. Her grip on Emmaline tightened. Emmaline was grateful and astonished, really, to be on the receiving end of such loyalty from someone who had known her for only an afternoon.

"I will unhand this little...urchin," he replied, looking disdainfully down at Emmaline. "And I will apologize to you, Miss Waters. You have my profuse apologies for being present for such an unfortunate showing in my establishment. For thievery is certainly no business for a fine lady such as yourself. However, I will not unhand the ring. It is my strict policy and duty to retain stolen items brought into my shop and to inform the authorities of the dirty business. Thieves will often attempt to sell their ill-gotten goods before apprehension, you know. They are a quick and nasty lot." His dark eyes pierced into Emmaline's, and she wanted to look away, but something about the darkness she saw there drew her attention.

Gwendolyn loosened her grip on Emmaline's hand only after Mr. Tally released her arm. Emmaline's gaze remained fixed on Mr. Tally, as Gwendolyn reached up and tightened her hat pins and pulled up her gloves, straightening herself up after the unfortunate encounter. Her movements also seemed to dismiss Mr. Tally, showing she was ready to move on from this unfortunate encounter.

"Very well, Mr. Tally," Gwendolyn said, "It makes no matter to me if you feel you must follow a silly formality. We shall follow our own, shall we not, Emmaline?"

Hearing her name, Emmaline pulled her eyes away from the direction of Mr. Tally with his dark and terrible eyes, and looked back up at Gwendolyn.

"Excuse me? I'm afraid I don't understand." Emmaline's voice sounded so very small to her own ears.

"We will leave the ring with Mr. Tally, as he seems to be forcing us to do."

Emmaline's head shook in small little movements back and forth a few times, and her voice trembled. "No. I can't leave it here. I can't."

"He is giving us no choice, is that not the case, Mr. Tally? You are giving us no choice but to leave this ring here?"

Emmaline's head snapped back toward the man, and he inclined his head in an exaggerated polite looking nod.

"Then we must leave it here and be on our own way, to report your ring stolen, by this jeweler here."

It seemed that Gwendolyn was playing some kind of game, but the golden ring was not something to play games with. Emmaline couldn't even imagine what the repercussions of losing this ring in this time might be. If she left the ring with Mr. Tally, then she may never get it back, which would surely break her grandfather's heart, for she recalled the way his voice had broken when he had spoken her grandmother's name earlier that day, back in the farmhouse when the ring had been in his hand. But even more so, she feared there must also be a great many other consequences for losing the ring in this time. Would Emmaline be able to complete her work as a storysmith without the ring? Would she be stuck in the past in a strange town, unable to return home without the ring's magic? No, she could not leave the ring with this creepy, cruel jeweler. She wouldn't, and just as she stamped her foot on the carpeted floor, and shouted, *No!*, she found she did not have a choice, for Mr. Tally turned and ran into his office and out the back door, taking the ring with him. Emmaline shivered with fury and fear, realizing she had just encountered a storychanger, and he had her ring.

Chapter Ten

Running

Gwendolyn barely managed to restrain Emmaline from chasing Mr. Tally, the child with tears in her eyes, shouting *No! No!* over and over again as she struggled to break free of Gwendolyn's grasp and run after the jeweler with the terrible, dark eyes who had stolen her ring.

"We will get the ring back. Hush! Hush, child! All will be well. Stop this. Stop this instant. All will be well. Emmaline! Emma-*line*!" Words were tumbling out of Gwendolyn's mouth as she held onto the panicking little girl. "I cannot let you go after him. He is clearly not a good man. A little girl has no place running after a mad man such as he. All will be well. Stop this. Be calm, Emmaline. Be calm! Be calm. Be calm..." And then Gwendolyn's voice changed, or, Emmaline thought, it actually sounded as if an echo was coming from behind it, as if a voice was repeating those two words along with Gwendolyn as she continued to recite them.

Be calm. Be calm. Be calm.

It was Susannah. Emmaline took in a shaky breath, trying to calm her sobs, and she concentrated on the echoing voice, hoping to hear it more clearly.

Be calm, Emmaline. Susannah's voice was clear and true and unmistakable.

Emmaline closed her eyes, looking into the darkness in her mind for a sign, waiting for a vision to show her where to go. Something, anything, to tell her what to do.

The voice spoke again.

It is only a ring.

She saw only the darkness behind her closed eyelids, but she heard Susannah clearly now, as she felt Gwendolyn's hold on her arms loosen.

All will be well. Remember what I told you. Use caution, Emmaline. Not everyone is on your side. Focus on the task that will be revealed to you. Focus on the story. The ring is a ring. Mourn the loss of it later if you want, but for now, do the work you are here to do. Remember, you will know storychangers when you see them. You heard it in his voice. You saw it in his eyes. You saw something dark there, and you were right. You knew. And you will know as the story continues. You will know them, and you must not follow them. Let the story lead you, not the storychangers. The ring brought you here, but now that you are here, look for the story itself. You will find your way. All will be well. Now, move on to a new scene. This is a celebration, after all. Go where people are celebrating. Go!

Susannah's voice disappeared, and Emmaline squeezed her eyes closed tighter, hoping to hear the words again if she listened closer and focused on the sounds rather than the sights in the world around her, but it was of no use. The voice was gone. The room was silent. She slowly opened her eyes and looked up into the rather alarmed face of Gwendolyn who, it seemed, was at a loss for words at Emmaline's odd behavior, for even considering the circumstances of the ring being stolen, Emmaline was behaving in a rather odd manner with her panicking, her silence, and her fretfully tight eye shutting.

"I'm sorry," Emmaline's voice was weak and a bit scratchy from her panicked screaming from only moments before.

This seemed to snap Gwendolyn back to attention.

"Dear girl," Gwendolyn said, her voice a whisper, motherly and comforting, or as Emmaline thought, perhaps even grandmotherly. In that moment, even with the intensity of the story unfolding around her, Emmaline thought that family really was a lovely thing, for she doubted if Gwendolyn's whispered words would have felt half so comforting from a stranger as they did coming from someone who was family. Emmaline was thankful that she was there with her.

And as if responding to Emmaline's thought, Susannah's voice came back to Emmaline's mind, though this time it was loud and authoritative. *You must leave her now. Your work is not with her.*

Emmaline had been thoroughly confused before, but now she was absolutely stunned. Wasn't she here to help Gwendolyn's fairy tale along? Why else would she have encountered her very own great-grandmother the moment she arrived in this time? The task of ensuring Gwendolyn's reacquaintance and marriage to Jonah was not finished. What else was she supposed to do in this town, in this time?

How Emmaline wished the terrible Mr. Tally had not stolen the ring. Had it still been in Emmaline's hand, she would have examined its color, listened for it to sing, touched her fingers to the beautiful stone and felt for warmth or coolness, a sign that she was to remain where she was or to go somewhere else, for surely the words she had just heard in Susannah's voice could not be true. How could she leave Gwendolyn's side just as she had discovered the comfort family can bring and when she knew of no one else to be on this adventure with. Where would she go? This world was strange enough for Emmaline, without a family member to cling to. And that was when it dawned on Emmaline: Maybe she wasn't here to be a fairy granddaughter. Maybe she liked that idea for herself, such a sweet and fun role to play; but, this wasn't her story to write. She was here to work, not to create, and so, she did what she somehow knew she had to do.

"Gwendolyn, thank you for your help. But I have to go."

And Emmaline turned on her heels, and she ran.

Emmaline was not a runner. She was not particularly athletic. Frankly, she was rather clumsy. So it was not such a big surprise or even a disappointment to her when she fell, landing hard on her knees and the palms of her hands as soon as she reached the next street over from the jewelry shop. Though she was not a runner, she was determined. Emmaline pushed herself up off the uneven stone sidewalk, quickly wiped the dirt from her hands and took off running again. So determined was she that she took no notice when the beautiful hat Gwendolyn loaned her flew from her head. She didn't have a plan. She just knew that running felt right. Isn't that what characters often did in her beloved storybooks back home, she reminded herself? Characters in stories were quick. They conquered, they discovered, they went on adventures, and they ran. She just hoped, as she heard her stiff shoes clicking against the stones, that she was running in the right direction, and that somehow she would run right to the place she was supposed to be. However, as she rounded another corner, and noticed that she had gotten away from the bustle of the downtown area, away from all of the food carts and colorful Founders Day Signs and the commotion of builders hammering last minute boards into the stage in the center of town, she was disappointed to see that there was no one around her. The town seemed to have come to an end. The buildings were replaced with grass, and just beyond the grass, there was a wooded area. The sun was not yet setting, but it wouldn't be long until the day grew darker. The light was a little bluish as it tends to be before sunset, and she didn't know if continuing to walk straight ahead and heading into the woods so near sunset was a comforting thought. Emmaline had never liked the darkness.

She stood at the spot where the neatly trimmed grass at the edge of town ended and the wilder, scraggly grass at the entrance of the woods began. She was still and quiet for some moments before taking a few small steps forward, stopping again, and placing her palm on the papery bark of a birch tree beside her. Emmaline stared into the shade of the woods. It was a peculiar place. The trees were full of leaves, shading the ground which held a tattered blanket of old leaves covering the spots between the solemn trunks of the oaks, birches, and pines. And there in the center of the woods was an opening. A narrow and long empty path, seemingly cleared out, leading the way away from the town and into the darkness. *Peculiar.* And just as Emmaline thought this word, a circle of light shone small and golden far down the path, deep into those woods, and she decided the path was meant for her. And she was not mistaken.

Chapter Eleven

In the Woods

She stepped into the woods. The path grew brighter, the golden circle of light growing and taking over more of the darkness of the shadowy woods, and just as she considered calling out and saying something like *Hello* or *Is anyone there?*, she heard someone call out to her.

"Hey, there!" It was a friendly voice, the voice of a child. And just as Emmaline understood that she was being spoken to, the light faded, and she stood looking at a boy about her age with a friendly smile on his face, his eyes blinking, as if he was adjusting to the sudden change in light.

"Hello." Emmaline responded with the only word she could muster at the moment. The strange light and the sudden absence of it had left her stunned.

"I'm hoping you'll say something smart. Because, I'll tell you what. I don't know what I ought to do next. And seeing that you're a kid with a shiny, new pair of shoes and a lost looking expression on your face, and seeing that I know what that means, well, seems like you might know something about what happens next."

"What happens next…" Emmaline repeated the boy's words, hoping they would make sense to her if she said them herself. However, that hope was not to come true, so she continued to stand there, wishing she knew what to do.

"You must be new," the boy reasoned.

"New?"

"Yeah, new. I remember being new and confused. Truth is, I'm still confused all the time." Here the boy laughed a little, which didn't do anything to lighten Emmaline's heart.

"Can we move out of the woods?"

"Now you're talking. Where are we headed? You got something figured out?" The boy seemed eager to get moving, and he began marching enthusiastically back up the clearing toward town.

"I would just like to get out of the woods, where the sun is still shining a little," Emmaline said as calmly as she could manage.

"Shucks. I thought you had a plan," he said, and halted his march back to town, walking back around in a circle toward Emmaline, but looking up at the shadowy forest canopy.

Emmaline stood silently for a moment, and her mind fixed upon a certain word the boy had said: *plan.* Emmaline stood next to an oak tree, her feet crunching down on dry leaves. She looked over at the boy and wondered who he was and if she should trust him with the things she knew.

He seemed to be about her age. He was dressed strangely, in a blue-striped shirt with a crisp collar and blue jeans that didn't seem quite right for this time in the world, but it was neat and plain enough to be not absolutely out of place. She looked down at his shoes and noticed how new and polished they looked and that they matched this era perfectly with their small little height added to the heel and the tiny little laces.

"Are you a…?" Emmaline began, but she couldn't bring herself to say the word "storysmith." She was new to this, and she didn't know all of the rules, all of the boundaries. However, it seemed like a good guideline not to mention the whole traveling-through-time, storysmithing thing to someone who was not a part of this adventure. So instead of speaking the word, she looked curiously at this boy, and waited to see if he would finish her sentence.

"Course I am!" was all he said. "Now, have you figured out your job yet, because far as I can tell, there wouldn't be two of us here at the same time unless this bit of storysmithing is a doozie. Usually, from what I've seen in my other two journeys, the usual way to get along with working a story is by yourself. Except for sometimes, when the storychangers start nosing around or when there's some kind of race to get things patched up quick. So, what's the job?"

Emmaline stood silently. She didn't know the job, of course. She had thought she knew, but having been told to leave Gwendolyn immediately, she was no longer sure of anything. She was lost, at the edge of the woods, with a stitch in her side from running, skinned up knees and burning palms from falling, and absolutely no clue what to do. Now, there was a boy standing there asking her what was next. Possibilities swam in her mind. Susannah hadn't said anything about other storysmiths. Emmaline considered that maybe this was something she was supposed to find out on her own. Or, maybe this would have been the sort of thing Susannah would have shared with her had it been true. So, it seemed possible in that moment that this little boy was lying. *He couldn't be a storysmith*, Emmaline thought. If she was to have a partner, then she would have been told that. Then again, hadn't Susannah told her something about not needing to know everything at once and that she would be given the knowledge she needed at the time she needed it? Yet, Emmaline thought, this little boy could be one of the bad guys Susannah had warned her about. He could be a storychanger. That seemed like something a storychanger would do once they identified a storysmith—try to thwart them with tricks and disguises. But then, the boy said the one thing that Emmaline needed to hear, the one thing that could have set her mind at ease in that moment, and the one thing that could have convinced her that he was a storysmith and that he was to be trusted.

"Things don't simply *happen*, now, do they? We better get to work."

"Right," Emmaline breathed out the word, goosebumps shivering over her arms. "Things do not simply happen. They are chosen."

The boy looked up at Emmaline, a strange expression on his face as if he didn't know what had turned her countenance so serious all of a sudden, then he blinked, went back to grinning and said, "Well, let's help them happen. What do you say?"

She nodded, a small smile lighting up her face. It did feel good to be in the presence of another child again. Adults were often so comforting and helpful to Emmaline, but really, there was something about someone her age to make the world seem a little lighter.

And she was certainly in need of a little lightening up at that moment.

"I'm Emmaline," she said, as the boy suddenly sat down on the ground and started removing things from a leather satchel he had been carrying over his shoulder.

"The name's James," he said. "You can call me 'Jimmy' though."

"Which do you prefer?"

"I just said you could call me 'Jimmy.'" He laughed and shook his head at her question, clearly finding her manners amusing.

"Right," Emmaline said. And then she thought to herself that perhaps this was part of the reason she had such an awkward and slow time of making friends, she often missed their meaning. She always tried to be so polite, so solicitous, but that generally came across as plain and simple awkwardness with the children she met.

"When are you from?" Emmaline asked.

"*Whew!*" He whistled, a long and high sound, and then shaking his head he said, "You sure are new, aren't ya? We can't talk to each other about things like that. What a mess that would make! Next thing you know, we start telling each other about our times and what's going on back home and what's happening in the world and all, and then the one from the farthest in the future starts giving hints to a fellow, or maybe to a gal, that he, or she, ought not to have. No, storysmiths talk about the time they are working in, not the time they are from."

"Oh," Emmaline said. "Right. Right! That does make sense."

He nodded, his expression serious, but his eyes twinkled a bit.

"How do you know this? Can I ask that?"

"You can ask anything. Don't know if I'll go answering it." Here he laughed, and Emmaline really was glad to hear that sound. "Same way as you are picking up things, I reckon. Just picked it up on the job. Course, I never did work with another storysmith before, so I didn't get answers from one of us, but you know, my pal from my resting spot, he told me lots, especially in the briefing I got at the end of my first job. Shoot, he told me all sorts of helpful stuff there. And then there was that nasty storychanger from my second job. He and I got into a real, genuine archery contest, if you can believe that, and he was so upset about losing that he ended up throwing an absolute fit and letting loose with all kinds of things about the way those guys work while he stood there trampling on his quiver of arrows. Shoot. He was a real mess, that one. Sore loser. Course most bad apples are sore losers, ain't that right?" He looked back up toward Emmaline, and she nodded once, but it was clear that her attention was now focused on the contents of his leather satchel, which Jimmy had been busily spreading out on the ground before them.

Emmaline sat down and reached out as if to touch the treasures, her hand unmoving in the air above them, her eyes looking to Jimmy, clearly waiting for permission.

"Go ahead," he nodded.

There was an old map made of something that looked much thicker and softer than paper. It reminded her of treasure maps she had seen in storybook illustrations. There was a silver pocket watch and a gold one. They were both large. She reached for the silver one, and turned her hand over, looking down at it in the palm of her hand. It was heavy and cold and beautiful, like something a wealthy man would have owned a hundred years ago, or Emmaline thought, perhaps like someone would have owned in the time she now found herself in. It was attached to a tarnished silver chain, and she pushed down on a little knob attached to the top of it and heard it click open. Inside there wasn't a clock at all, but a smooth, black surface with small letters elegantly formed on it, spelling out the instruction: *Find another smith. Run.*

Emmaline touched the letters and gasped. As she ran her fingers across the letters, she smudged part of the phrase away. It seemed that the writing was done in chalk. It was a little chalkboard inside a pocketwatch.

"Oh, that's okay. I'm done with that one anyway," Jimmy shrugged, and reaching for the pocketwatch, which wasn't actually a watch, he wiped away the remaining part of the message.

"Was that message about me?" asked Emmaline, her eyes still fixed on the curious treasure.

"Course it was," he laughed. "Why else would I go chasing after a strange girl? Right when it told me to run, there you were, running like you couldn't get to somewhere fast enough, so I figured I was to follow you, but you were pretty fast, so I came in through the side of the woods and thought I could cut you off that way. It worked. And now, here we are. That's what pocket scripts are for. These here things are just about as handy as a pocket on a shirt, or a skirt, I reckon. I was gifted them both after my first assignment. Wasn't real sure what to do with two pocket scripts. I have only ever had messages written on the silver one you have there. The gold one hasn't worked for me yet."

Jimmy pursed his lips, squinted his eyes a bit, and tilted his head to the side as he looked down at the gold pocket script with its light and beautiful chain. He plucked it up from the ground, held it out to Emmaline and said, "Maybe it isn't mine. Here."

Emmaline's response was a low whisper. "Truly? You want me to have it?" The pocket script was not only beautiful and old and just the sort of thing she would love to own, but it was also magical and useful all at once, it seemed, and that made it the sort of thing she would treasure forever.

"Maybe it'll be of use to you. And me, too, really, if we are working on this together."

Emmaline gently wrapped her fingers around the cold case, and whispered, "Thank you."

"Now I can't guarantee it'll work. Hasn't worked for me yet, like I said. It's worth a shot though."

"How does it work?"

"Now that I can't tell you. Whenever I find myself lost or wondering what I'm to do next on an assignment, I take out the pocket script and check for a new message on the blackboard inside. Sometimes there is a message, sometimes there isn't. Remember now: We don't make the plans, we just work for the one who does. So you have a question, maybe you'll get an answer, maybe you won't. Sometimes you getting an answer can be part of the plan, part of the story, sometimes not. But it's okay to keep asking, either way. Asking doesn't get in the way of anything."

"I see," Emmaline said, though she was only just starting to grasp onto how storysmithing worked.

"And who is the one who made the story? Can you tell me that? My guide couldn't really tell me when I asked."

"I don't know. But whoever it is, that person knows us. That's for sure."

Emmaline considered this for a moment and then, not really knowing what to think of it all, she continued to look through the treasures. There were several rocks, all small, but of various shapes and shades of grey and black; a harmonica; several pencils; two shiny, green apples; and a small, wooden box. She reached for the box. It looked well polished and quite new, and when she snapped it open, she gasped.

"It's a ring box," Jimmy said, grabbing up one of the apples and taking a large bite, chewing it with an open mouth as he spoke. "Now that...I have no idea what to make of. I picked it up when I followed the map. It was sitting there on a park bench right where "X" marked a spot on the map. So, I picked it up, felt okay about it, you know, got the full bellied, comfortable feeling you get when you're doing the right thing, and I put it in the bag. You know what to make of it?" He looked at Emmaline quizzically and offered her the other apple. She smiled her thanks, but gestured "no" with a small wave of her hand, feeling too excited to eat.

Emmaline answered, "I think it means we need to get my ring back now. I guess it wasn't time before to worry about the ring, but now that you're here, maybe it's time to go looking for it."

"Good thing you know."

"It's my grandmother's ring," she said. "And it's how I got here."

"Well, don't worry about the getting-you-here part; getting back is the best kind of fun of this whole job. You sure don't get out of here the same way you came. But I reckon we still better find that ring and fast. I learned the hard way on my first job. The things that transport us can become real dangerous in the hands of the wrong people. If we don't get that ring back in time, there could be real trouble. Come on," he said, taking the last bite of his apple and pitching the core deeper into the woods. He grabbed her arm and pulled her up, not unkindly, but not at all gently, and it made Emmaline wonder if this was what having a brother would feel like. She had always wanted a brother. Or a sister. Or a cousin. Someone. Living in her house was so lonely, with only her mom and her dad and that cat, who were all so occupied with their own concerns lately.

She stamped her feet, physically snapping herself back to attention and to focusing on the work of the moment.

"You said 'dangerous?'" Emmaline asked.

"I did."

"What do you mean 'dangerous?'"

"You don't want to find out," Jimmy said, shaking his head, reaching up to make sure his sand-colored hair was still neatly in place.

"I don't see how being vague can help now. Tell me." Emmaline surprised herself with the amount of authority she heard in the tone of her own voice.

Jimmy seemed to be surprised, too. His eyes widened a bit and he reached up to tidy his hair again, a gesture Emmaline recognized as a nervous habit, rather than an actual desire to straighten his hair.

"Okay, well. Here's the thing about your ring. It had to belong to a storysmith before you. Probably someone from your family. Storysmithing runs in families, you know."

"No, I didn't know." Emmaline's mind started spinning, imagining who in her family might also be a storysmith or might have been one before her.

"Course it does. So you said this ring was your grandmother's? Well, there you go. Your grandmother must have been a storysmith. The story goes like this: A storysmith must leave something behind for the next storysmith to come along in the family. As soon as that thing is given to the new storysmith, the role of storysmith begins again. Your grandmother left you her ring, and as soon as it was given to you, you were swept away to become a storysmith. That sound about right?"

"Yes, that's just how it happened, I suppose."

"Right. Well, my Uncle Granger left me a harmonica. Soon as I brought it to my lips and tried to play it, well, I was swept away myself." Jimmy nodded his head down toward where the harmonica rested on the ground. "It was a terror to get back, and before I did, there were more than a few holes burned into the ground."

"Holes burned in the ground?" Emmaline asked, looking sharply at Jimmy, a scared, burning feeling tumbling up from her stomach to her throat.

She thought of the hole she had seen in the ground back near her mother's herb garden.

Jimmy quickly packed his treasures back into his satchel, then stood up and said, "That's right. Holes burned in the ground. You ready?"

"I think so."

"And you still have no clue where we ought to be going?"

"No…" was Emmaline's reply as she pondered. Emmaline thought after the word left her mouth: She did have a clue. She did. She had Susannah's words from back at the jewelry shop. So, she shook her head a little as if to shake away the response she had just given, and she spoke again, and this time said, "Yes, this is a celebration. We should go somewhere people are celebrating."

Jimmy smiled. "Sounds good to me."

Emmaline stepped out of the woods with her new friend or, at least, her new storysmithing companion. Her ring was missing. She had not discovered what she was to do in this place and time, but it did feel good not to be alone on this adventure anymore. She smoothed her yellow skirt, looked over at

Jimmy as he looked curiously back in the direction of the town. He did seem like a nice kid, she thought. Maybe she *would* make a friend this summer. Emmaline smiled. She did not let Jimmy see the smile. Emmaline thought that boys were not as fond of smiling and talking about friendship as girls tended to be. While that generalization may have applied to some boys, she couldn't have been further from the truth in this case: Jimmy was a great fan of smiling.

Chapter Twelve

Blackbirds

Emmaline and Jimmy, each glad to have found the other, were walking toward the center of town, right to the heart of the preparations for the celebration, when rain began to fall. It was the kind of rain that fell in heavy drops that plopped down on you with little splashes on your arms and face. Drops of rain slid down Emmaline's ankles and into her shoes, where they were stiff and open at the back of her foot. The rain by itself was not such an astonishing thing. Rain may fall when and where it falls, whether a girl is living out an ordinary kind of summer on a farm, or if she is back in time on some kind of adventure during a second summer. But, the presence of such a hearty rain made what Emmaline saw next astonishing and terrible. Just as puddles began to form in uneven parts of the cobblestone streets where Emmaline and Jimmy were making their way back toward town, hoping to find some sign of what they should do next, a fire started in the middle of the street, right in front of Emmaline's clickety-clackety, rain-soaked shoes.

"Oh!" Emmaline shrieked, her hands thrown out to her sides to find balance and steady herself, as she stopped short of entering the sudden burst of flame.

"Careful!" Jimmy said, reaching out to Emmaline. "Oh, boy. It's started."

Emmaline looked down at the burning ground and saw no sign of what could have started the fire, or what was burning, but there was nothing to support the flames, no pieces of wood, no leaves, only the ground itself, which had been soaked with rain water and showed no sign of having a reason or way to be burning. And then, almost as quickly as the fire had started, it died down, leaving a hole in the ground, a dark, deep pit that seemed to have nothing in it. The ground had simply burned, and now there was a hole. She could see this mysterious hole in the earth clearly enough that there was no mistaking it, unlike that one that had burned in her front yard. Emmaline recalled what Jimmy had said about holes burning only a few moments before.

"Is this because of my ring?"

"This is because of storychangers. I told you the thing that brought you here would have power. I bet they have it and are causing trouble. Those holes are a sure sign storychangers are trying to mess with the story, making changes. We have to get your ring back."

Jimmy grabbed on to Emmaline's wrist and started running. He tried to explain as they ran, but it was hard for Emmaline to make out his words as they tumbled out of him in a breathless tangle.

"Storychangers usually just have little things…they can do. Make someone late for an appointment. Change the way…a scene…plays out…moving things around…when they get…hands on magic…magic changes everything. They can…burn holes in the story…in the story itself. We gotta…we gotta stop them."

"What if…" Emmaline grabbed onto her side as she ran, the pain stabbing at her partly from running so quickly, and partly, she thought, from the fear shooting through her, for the flames burning the ground away right in front of her was the most terrifying thing she had ever seen. "What if we can't?"

"What if we can?" Jimmy said, and he stopped running and flashed a smile.

Now this, thought Emmaline, *is why he's here.* Emmaline Hazeltree may get things done, she may be sensible and organized and good, but daring and hopeful she had never been. It seemed they might be a good team. Or, at least, he would be a help to her. For this may have been the point in the story when Emmaline would have needed a rest, maybe when she would have cried out in hopes that Susannah would help her find her Place of Stillness, and Emmaline would take a break to talk some things out. But no, Jimmy inspired her to keep going.

He was looking at something up ahead. They stood, both of them catching their breath, Emmaline looking at Jimmy, trying to figure out what he was focusing on, since she had seen nothing in the distance. They had reached the middle of town. Preparations for the Founders Day Celebration were still in full swing with vendors and carts, streamers and signs all around. Children were standing on the sidewalks pointing and laughing. Women wearing black dresses with white aprons walked through town carrying baskets full of produce. Everything looked happy and exciting, and nothing looked like things were amiss, like holes were burning in the ground, where people walked, where they lived, where their stories took place. Nothing looked wrong, except for one thing, and Jimmy had found it: Straight ahead, just at the corner of Main Street, stood a young man talking to a line of large, shiny blackbirds. And those birds stood attending to the man, as if they were listening to him.

"That's our man."

"The one with the birds?" Emmaline wondered, taking a step forward.

"Yep. He'll have your ring alright. He's got some kind of mischief going with the animal world now, looks like. And that sounds like magic to me. He isn't playing by any kind of regular rules. We get him, we get your ring. But first," he said, taking a few steps forward to stand in front of Emmaline and halt her process forward, "we watch."

"Watch?" Just as the word left Emmaline's mouth, another circle of fire blazed up to her right, burning a hole quickly into the ground and then dying down. She turned back to the crowd of people behind her, looking to see if anyone had noticed, and it seemed they had not. It could not be long, Emmaline thought, until they did start to notice actual pits popping up on Main Street. And then what kind of chaos would ensue, she wondered?

"We need to get the ring now," she said.

"No," Jimmy said, adjusting the satchel on his shoulder, pushing it further behind him and letting out an exaggerated sigh. "We watch. He is working against the story. We are working for it, but we don't know what we are doing yet, which means this is what you call a 'defense situation.'"

"Defense?"

"Yes, like in football. Or whatever kind of sport you have back home. Sometimes we work to make things happen, and sometimes we work to stop storychangers from changing the way things happen. Seeing as how neither you or I know what we are doing at the moment, we are stuck playing defense, and we need to watch that creepy guy with the birds there." Jimmy glanced back over his shoulder where the man stood, still talking to a line of blackbirds. "And whatever it is he is doing, we watch until we understand his goal, and then we squash it."

"That does seem to make sense," Emmaline said, her eyes narrowing as she watched the man.

"Yep," Jimmy said.

And it really was a good thing that Emmaline and Jimmy had agreed on this course of action, because at this exact moment, something happened, something that was a clear sign of what the storychanger was trying to change. A low roaring and ruffling of the birds' wings sounded ahead, and the birds all took flight at once and headed toward Main Street, where Emmaline and Jimmy stood. They flew straight ahead creating a dark and wavy shadow above the children, above the town, and then they swooped down all at once and flew into the open windows of the large, brick school building, the same school building Gwendolyn Waters had stomped out of so angrily when Emmaline had first encountered her. There were a few shrieks from women in town who had witnessed the strange occurrence. But mostly there was silence as the vendors, the basket-holding women, the families, the children, as everyone stared toward the school building to behold a flock of thirty to forty blackbirds fly into its windows. Moments of silence continued to tick by, and then it came: ear-splitting screams from young and older children; both front doors being thrown open; a boarding school full of students running to escape, their arms covering their heads that were ducked low on their shoulders, shielding themselves from the birds flying close by them and back out of the school. It looked as if the birds were chasing the children away, and of course, Emmaline and Jimmy realized, this was exactly what they must have been doing. Yet, they had no idea why.

And then—*whoosh!*—another hole burned into the ground just behind Emmaline, and she had to hop forward to move away from the sudden swirl of heat she felt at her feet.

"We need to get into that school," Emmaline heard the words leave her, before she even decided to actually say them. But, as soon as she heard them leave her mouth, she knew, utterly and absolutely, that they were true.

She reached into the pocket of her yellow skirt, even in that terrifying moment, she found herself capable of appreciating the sensibleness of a skirt with pockets. She closed her eyes and whispered, "Please," hoping for something that was absolutely not sensible in the least. Though she was and had always been the most sensible of girls, Emmaline, at this point in the story, was learning to seek out something beyond what seemed to make sense. And then she pressed down on the little peg at the top of the pocket script, opened her eyes, and saw a message, neatly written on the little circle of blackboard inside. Only two words were there, but it was all she needed in that moment, for the message was a purpose, and that is what a storysmith needs, and she felt, for the first time on that whirlwind of a day, like she was truly a storysmith. Maybe it was the holes burning around her, maybe it was the anger that flooded into her as she saw the young man who surely had her grandmother's ring, maybe it was the frantic look on the faces of the school children as they ran, or maybe it was simply the way her heart was beating, strong and steady, as she held on to that pocket script and realized that it had been meant for her, that she wasn't alone, and that this was her role to play. But whatever it was, she whispered, to the invisible writer of the message, "Thank you," as she stared down at those two words:

Find Cecille.

Emmaline snapped the pocket script closed, tucked it into her skirt pocket, grabbed on to Jimmy's wrist, and said, "Let's go."

She headed up the school's exterior stairs, opened the doors and said, "Hello? Hello?" She called again and again, gently but loudly, as she and Jimmy walked from one large room to the next, up the stairs and back down. It was a vast and beautiful school, with high ceilings and polished oak desks. But, something was strange about it, and Emmaline could not quite figure out what it was. Jimmy figured it out rather quickly.

"What kind of school doesn't have any books?" he asked.

And he was right. Emmaline knew it was a school only because she had noticed the sign on the door earlier that morning, she had seen the uniforms of the children, and she had heard Gwendolyn talk about the school. Yet, now that she was standing inside, she saw that Jimmy was correct. There were no books. There was no globe, and there were no maps on the walls. There was a large blackboard at the end of the largest room on the main floor of the building, but it stood clean and blank, with no sign of chalk or chalk dust anywhere. The room smelled clean, of vinegar and lemon oil. It was lovely, but it was empty.

Emmaline called out, "Cecille? Hello?"

But no answer came.

Chapter Thirteen

The Necessary School

Emmaline headed toward the stairs to search the second floor again. She trusted her feeling that she was in the right place. This time, she decided, she would take her time and make a careful search, paying attention to the details.

Jimmy's attention went from the left to the right of the great hallway on the first floor. Finding no sign of anyone, he called out to Emmaline, "I'll look in the kitchen, then see if there's a basement. Meet you back here in a few minutes unless I yell for you or you yell for me. Okay?"

"Okay," Emmaline responded, already stepping slowly but surely onto the staircase.

The wooden stairs were narrow, polished and shiny. The whole school, not just the classroom, was immaculate, from the shining stairs, to the clear window panes, to the dust-free ceilings. It really was a wonder that so many children spent their days in a building, and yet it remained so clean and perfectly kempt.

When she reached the top step, she noticed two gold-plated plaques posted on the wall. One saying "BOYS" with an arrow pointing toward the right, and one saying "GIRLS" with an arrow pointing toward the left. Emmaline, in search of someone named "Cecille," went left.

Emmaline stepped into a large, open room with two rows of iron beds painted white, all covered neatly with blue and white striped blankets. There were no pillows on the beds, and each bed had its own desk beside it with a big lamp at its center. Still, no books, no paper nor pencils, there was nothing to indicate that this was a school anywhere to be seen. Above the head of each bed was a small, framed blackboard hanging by a piece of thick twine. On each blackboard was written a name, and on the very last bed in the first row was written the name "Cecille."

Cecille's bed, desk, and lamp looked like all of the others, but when Emmaline opened the small drawer of the desk, she thought what she found inside was surely different than what must have been in all of the other desks. It did not at all appear to be the work of a child. Inside the desk drawer was a set of blueprints for what looked like some sort of machine. The design was elaborate, precisely organized and richly detailed. Emmaline was not a designer, an architect, nor an engineer, or whatever one must be to understand the plans on the papers in front of her; she couldn't fully understand what she was looking at. What she did know was that in the very corner of the largest piece of paper she unrolled from the desk drawer, a paper on which was drawn some sort of ship or rocket or some

144

such, was written "Cecille's Design, for journeying to the Moon, and perhaps to the planet Mars."

"Well, this is curious," Emmaline said to herself, letting herself fall down into the plain, wooden chair at Cecille's desk.

Before Emmaline had more than a moment to think about what this might mean, she was startled by the sound of footsteps, rather loud ones, coming down the hallway in her direction.

Emmaline shut the desk drawer quietly, her eyes darting around the room, looking for curtains to dart behind, or perhaps a closet to hide in. It was no use. Emmaline looked back to the room's doorway just in time to see a woman wearing a black dress, a mean-looking frown, and a hat with a large red feather poking up from the side at a fierce angle. The woman stepped into the room, placed her hands on her hips and said, "Who are you and where are my children?"

"Excuse me, ma'am." *Now is the time to think fast, Emmaline*, she thought to herself. "I don't know where the children are," Emmaline responded, thankful yet again, that she could speak the truth while not speaking too much.

The woman squared her shoulders, her rather high shoulders thanks to the heavily padded dark jacket she was wearing, and she narrowed her eyes, waiting, or rather, Emmaline thought, daring her to continue to speak.

"I saw them run away, and I thought maybe I could help."

"I see," the woman said.

Though, she probably did not see, Emmaline Hazeltree thought to herself, for how could anyone, in such strange circumstances, see what was happening?

"I rather thought they were over trying to run away," the woman said before clenching her teeth in such a fierce manner that Emmaline saw the muscles along her jaw twitch.

"Is this…is this a school?"

"What a question to ask. Can you not read the signage, child? Or course this is a school—the finest in Watertown. And who is asking? You have not told your name."

"I'm sorry. I'm…I am Emmaline. I'm…I'm a relation of the Waters family," Emmaline spoke quickly, without thinking if this was wise or not, for while the

Waters name may protect her in the moment, it may expose her in some way or complicate her circumstance; explaining the nature of her relation to the Waters family wouldn't exactly be simple. But alas, she had spoken the name before deciding, so she must stick to it.

"Well, that does change the situation. Perhaps you are here about the small matter of the novels the young Miss Waters had hoped to donate earlier today?"

Emmaline said nothing, only smiled.

"You see, we are a rather…modern school here, and we find no need for works which remove the focus of our pupils from hard work and obedience and the real stuff of life. Novels tend to distract children with imagination, creativity, the fancies of science, and other such useless endeavors. My pupils are here to learn, Miss…Miss Waters," she spoke the name "Waters" as if it was the sweetest word in the dictionary, yet Emmaline could tell that this woman had no love for that name, or for anything good, so it seemed to Emmaline. She looked like the sort of woman who would squash the light out of anything she could, with the set of her jaw, her narrow eyes, and the way she spoke about her students.

"And what is it you learn here, Miss…I'm sorry, I do not know your name?" Emmaline asked, as sweetly as she could manage.

"Mistress Rottenden," she said, nodding her head in a regal manner, as if she had just spoken the Queen's name. "We learn what is necessary. The children who study here will grow up to meld well into the world. We pride ourselves on that. There will be no outliers grown here."

And then it clicked. It clicked so clearly in Emmaline's head, that she practically heard the sound in her mind of a key fitting into place and turning, opening up the truth of something. She needed to find this Cecille. She needed to get her out of this "necessary" school. Cecille was only a child now, like Emmaline, but it was clear from her notebooks and blueprints that she was destined for something much greater than what was "necessary" according to Mistress Rottenden. Emmaline knew, as she stood staring into the cold, stern eyes of this Mistress Rottenden, that if she did not get Cecille out of this book-less and comfortless and imagination-squashing school, then maybe the light inside of Cecille wouldn't grow strong, and someone or something would be able to stop her, to uninspire her, to squash her imagination.

That's it, Emmaline thought. *I must find Cecille, and I must get her away from this place.*

Chapter Fourteen

Storychangers

Emmaline turned and left the room, offering no explanation to the Mistress of the School. She raced down the stairs, pushing against the banister to keep herself from falling as she took the narrow stairs two at a time. When she reached the bottom she ran into

Jimmy, who was standing nervously at the foot of the stairs.

"Who's the lady?" he asked, looking up to where Mistress Rottenden stood, her face holding the same menacing look it had when speaking with Emmaline. The mistress of the Necessary School stood glaring down at him, regarding him, though he was just a boy, as an enemy.

"The head mistress here," Emmaline explained. "Come on, we have to find those kids."

Jimmy smiled, a full smile that took over his face. He smoothed down his already neat hair, straightened his somehow-still-crisp collar, and said, "You've got a plan."

"I think…I think I know why we're here," Emmaline said, exiting through the large doors of the Necessary School, looking back and forth down the street, trying to decide which way to go. "No, I don't think I know," she shook her head, as she changed her mind, changed her words, "I am certain I know why we are here. I don't know how I know. I just know." She smiled. It felt good to smile after being in that school, she realized, like her joy could erase some of its drabness.

"Good. That's good!" Jimmy reached into his leather satchel and pulled out his map. "You've got to trust those feelings here. Your resting spot person told you that, right? To trust your feelings?"

"Yes, she did." Emmaline thought of Susannah. Just the thought of her dear friend calmed her racing heart a bit and helped her to take a deep breath and get a good sense of the plan taking shape in her mind.

Emmaline looked over at Jimmy who was staring intently at the map she had seen earlier in the woods with his other treasures—the map on the thin, soft material, the one that resembled her idea of a treasure map.

Her eyes must have asked her question, because before she even expressed it, Jimmy answered, "Sometimes a map doesn't work until you know where you're going."

Emmaline laughed, thinking of the coffee-stained maps in the back seat of her parents' car and realizing that Jimmy's words were exactly true. The red and blue tangles and curves on those maps never meant much at all to her until she knew the spot where they were headed. Once she knew that, she knew how to use the map to get there. Of course, at this point in the story, Emmaline Hazeltree hoped that the map Jimmy held in his hand would be even more helpful, perhaps even a little magical. And she was not to be disappointed. As she and Jimmy looked down at the map, the landmarks on it, the buildings, the forests, the roads, and the letters all swirled around until the map looked like a colorful bowl of paint being stirred into a liquid rainbow. And then the colors all separated again and formed a neat picture of landmarks, buildings, and trees. What had once been a busy tangle of unfamiliar landscapes and roads and paths and buildings was now a map labeled "WATERTOWN." There was Main Street, there was the Necessary School, there was the Waters house, the park, the wooded area at the edge of town, and there, right in the middle of the map, was a picture of an hourglass.

"Oh!" Emmaline exclaimed, remembering the tiny crystal hourglass folded into her skirt pocket. She pulled out the hourglass, held it in her hand. The violet sand sparkled and swiftly fell through to the bottom chamber, and floating there in the top chamber, where the sand had once hidden it, was a golden arrow pointing to the right. And the children knew this was the direction they were to go.

Emmaline and Jimmy put away the map and the hourglass. Both of the children were absolutely giddy. They had arrived at the part of storysmithing which was the most fun, the most exciting. They were about to reach their goal, they were about to find the person they knew they must find, and they knew where to find her. As they took off running, watching the cobblestone street as they ran, hopping over two holes that had been burned in the ground, Emmaline remembered her father's instructions to have an adventure this summer.

I am, dad, she thought. *I am having an adventure!*

The streets were clear of most of the people now. Some of them had gone in search of the children. Some had run to their homes and locked the doors and closed the shutters after seeing such a fright. Though thankfully, this was only a small few, for most of the witnesses to the event had convinced themselves that their eyes had been playing tricks on them, as people often do when extraordinary things occur right in front of them. This refusal to believe in the extraordinary did make the scene much less chaotic and gave the storysmiths more clearance to do their work. Panic and chaos do tend to make things much more difficult.

The children hadn't been running long, down no more than four blocks, when they saw her. She was a small girl, maybe six or seven years old, and she was huddled in the dotted shade of a young cherry tree, which had been planted on the corner of a smallish side street.

They both stopped running at the same moment, both of them knowing two things: First, if this little girl was Cecille, the one they were to find, then they must not scare her away; and second, if they were on the right path, then the storychanger must certainly be nearby, possibly setting a trap, possibly waiting to pounce, or maybe, just waiting on their next move, whatever that may be.

Jimmy spoke to the little girl first. "Are you Cecille?" he asked, already believing he knew the answer. She had been sitting in the exact direction the hourglass's arrow had pointed, and he and Emmaline had both caught sight of her and stopped running at once. Emmaline again consulted the hourglass, to be sure. The tiny, golden arrow was now trembling excitedly and was pointing directly at the little girl.

The child looked up, her eyes wide with fright, her hair full of dark curls that fell down over her eyes. She pushed them back and waited for the two children in front of her to say more.

"Where are your parents?" Emmaline asked. Seeing that she and Jimmy needed to get the girl out of that terrible school, it seemed that the most sensible route was to locate her parents, to try to convince them to take her home, or at least to a new boarding school, one with books and globes and kind teachers.

"I don't know. I think I don't have any," she replied, and her voice wavered, but then she brought her shoulders up and jutted out her chin in a way that showed Emmaline that she was determined to be strong in her life, despite her circumstances, and despite her young age. It really was an amazing thing, Emmaline thought, this young child's strength in the face of her adversity, her intelligence in the absence of a good education, her defiance of Mistress Rottenden, while having no parents to run home to.

Emmaline didn't know what to do. She felt helpless, utterly helpless, for a moment, and then she remembered the pocket script. She pulled it out of her pocket and pushed it open. But, the little blackboard was empty.

A few steps away, another hole burned in the ground. Cecille's eyes widened, but she didn't shrink away.

"I want to help you," Emmaline said, "but I'm not sure how."

"Could you...could you help me find my uncle?"

"Your uncle? You have an uncle!" Emmaline almost cried with relief, hearing that this little girl did have family.

"Yes, yes we can do that," Emmaline said, "Can't we, Jimmy?"

"Sure thing," he said, pulling out the last shiny apple from his satchel and holding it out to Cecille.

She smiled and took the apple.

Emmaline decided Jimmy must have a little sister back home, for he seemed to know just what to do to put the little girl at ease.

"Do you know your uncle's name?" Emmaline asked.

"Yes. It is Jonah Hazeltree."

Emmaline laughed. She threw her head back and laughed, and then, when Jimmy looked at her as if she had lost her senses, she leaned over and whispered to him, "Jonah Hazeltree is my great-grandfather. I saw him this morning. And…"

Jimmy stood waiting on her next words, and when they didn't come in time for him, he asked, "And what?"

"And he just got a job with the mapmaker in town. Find that mapmaker's office, and we'll find him. Hurry before the sun sets. He'll probably be off to watch the fireworks with everyone else tonight; it will be harder to find him in the crowd and, since he is new in town, no one will know who it is we are looking for. Let's go and see if we can catch him at work, or we'll surely have a much harder time of finding him…Let's go!"

"Let's beat feet!" Jimmy yelled.

But before the two storysmiths could take another step, a man stepped in their path. Emmaline recognized his posture and the long, black coat and realized that this was the same man who had bought Gwendolyn the lemon ice earlier that day, before Jonah had come along and bought her another. Of course, that man had been a storychanger, Emmaline now realized to herself. He had not wanted Jonah to buy Gwendolyn the lemon ice. He didn't want any part of the story to go as planned if he could help it. And now, she knew, this storychanger would not want her to help this child, Cecille, to be rescued from the drab reality of Mistress Rottenden's school. He didn't want her to realize the future that was planned for her.

"A trade?" the man asked. He looked much older than he had before, his skin showing wrinkles that looked like little scars on his face, but the darkness in his eyes almost sparkled.

"No trades," Jimmy said.

"Come now. I can give you a beautiful ring that, I know, you are very fond of indeed. In exchange, all I ask is that you allow me to escort this lost, little girl back to her school and head mistress. Surely, she would be safer in my company, rather than with two other lost children who seem to be in continuous danger of falling into holes in the ground, don't you agree?" The man reached into his pocket and pulled out Emmaline's grandmother's golden ring with the sea-colored gem set in the middle. He held it out to her, so gently and lightly, that it looked as if she could easily reach out and pluck it from his hand, but something held her back, kept her in place, and at a distance from this man.

And then Emmaline thought that maybe she heard the voice of Susannah in her mind saying, *Do not take anything from him. Nothing.* Or maybe it was her own voice, Emmaline only knew that she trusted the message. She was terrified not to trust it. However, she considered, it was her ring after all. And, Jimmy told her that they needed to get it back. But, no. She would take nothing from him, she decided. *Nothing.*

"I see," the man said.

"Sir," it was a tiny voice that came from behind Emmaline and Jimmy. The man craned his neck to see Cecille. "Would you like an apple?" she said.

And before Emmaline even thought to get in the way, before Jimmy thought to step between the little girl and the storychanger, Cecille held the shiny, green apple in the palm of her hand out to him. The storychanger, surprised by this child's bold gesture, and feeling confident that he was gaining the child's confidence, smiled, and plucked the apple from her hand.

"Ah!" he yelled, jerking his hand back from the apple as if he had been burned, and in that instant, Emmaline and Jimmy acted quickly. As the storychanger stumbled back, seemingly burned by the apple, he loosened his grip on the ring, and Emmaline caught it before it hit the ground, which caused her to smile with delight. Emmaline couldn't recall ever catching anything before. But, she tried when it counted, and she did it.

Just a few steps away, Jimmy was focused on getting Cecille far from the storychanger. He took her by the hand, and they began running before the storychanger had even regained his footing, as he shook his hand in the air, trying to calm its burning.

Emmaline saw Jimmy, with the hand that wasn't holding onto the running Cecille, reach into his satchel, retrieve the map, shake it open, and hold it up so he could view it while running. Emmaline had a feeling that all would be well and that she was, at least for now, safe from this storychanger. And it seemed, the storychanger must have known this, too. He looked down at her. His eyes were as dark as ever, but his expression had changed. He didn't look angry, but wary—terribly wary, like a hunted animal, like one who knew he had failed and was at some kind of an end. And this end, judging by the storychanger's face, could not be a good one.

The two stood there staring at one another, the storychanger with his burned hand, now cradled in his other hand. And Emmaline felt a calm settle over her as she stood there, holding her grandmother's ring in a tight grasp, but also holding it out in front of her a bit, so that the storychanger would not forget that she had the magic ring now, not he.

Suddenly they heard the roaring flapping of the blackbirds' wings. Both of them looked up as the flock, now grown to many hundreds, swooped down and landed on the ground. They encircled the wary storychanger and the young storysmith.

Emmaline knew something important should happen now, perhaps some kind of reckoning, perhaps some kind of agreement or argument. She had no idea what. She only knew that she had the ring, so she hoped he had no more magic to use. She thought that maybe she should talk to the blackbirds, to ask them to help her, to carry the storychanger away, but that did not feel right. And then she thought that maybe she should just tell the man to leave, but that did not seem right to her either. And then he spoke.

"There's always another chapter," he said, and then he shrugged his shoulders, pulled one side of his coat up to cover his anguished face, and then, he vanished. And, in the moment he vanished, the flock of blackbirds ascended and flew out of sight.

But before Emmaline Hazeltree let out a ragged sigh of relief, before she could turn around and decide which way to step next, before she could even smooth down her pretty yellow skirt, as was her habit, something moved in the corner of her field of vision. Or rather, someone moved, and she knew, she absolutely knew without even turning to focus in on him: It was Mr. Tally.

It was true that he no longer had her ring. At some point he had relinquished it to the now-vanquished storychanger, and the ring was safely with

Emmaline in the moment Mr. Tally ran past. And it was true that he seemed to be running away from her, so it might seem reasonable for Emmaline just to let him go, so she could then move on and find Jimmy or pat herself on the back for a job well done. Yet, something about him made her think twice, and Emmaline had learned to trust her instincts, so she took a deep breath, and she took off running, again, in the direction of Mr. Tally.

She did not need to run far. Mr. Tally, it seemed, did not like the idea of being chased, because he turned immediately to face Emmaline. And, unlike the first storychanger, Mr. Tally was on the offensive, ready to bend Emmaline's story to his own will. He was not offering any agreements. Instead, he offered a warning.

"You cannot, little girl, be in two places at once. Of course, neither can I. I have just been to the mapmaker's shop where Jonah Hazeltree has been employed. I left him a note. A sad, little note. And, I signed it in the name of your great-grandmother. It seems, or so the note says, that she will not meet him at the fireworks, and she would prefer that he not speak to her again, for they are two people from different worlds, and she is not likely to converse with him in the future. So, now you know this. And, either you run and steal that note from Jonah's desk before he sees it, or you follow me and try to stop me from taking Cecille back to the Necessary School where she belongs. Mistress Rottenden is a lovely lady and misses her pupil very much, I'm sure. So…run to Jonah's office and play fairy matchmaker, or try, if you can, to stop me from returning Cecille, but you can't do both. You must fail." Here he let forth a wicked laugh, grumbling low and empty of joy. "Think, girl. Without the proper care, Cecille won't make it to her next stop in the…story," his voice whispered the word "story," as if he feared it. His eyes darted back and forth after it passed his lips. "And, if you don't get that note before Jonah Hazeltree does, then your great-grandmother's story will certainly change. Won't it?"

Emmaline Hazeltree felt her feet press hard into the ground. She didn't know what to say, what move to make, and it took a great deal of effort to try to remain steady until she decided what to do next.

Mr. Tally smiled a slow, crooked smile and said, "Which part of the story will it be? You choose. Which matters most to you? Your family's story? Or Cecille's?"

A very small voice inside her mind, whispered, *Don't. Don't choose.* But she heard louder thoughts moving back and forth in her head. *Your great-grandmother*, they said. *Go to her, go to her. This is about your own family now! Go! You aren't even sure why you are getting the little girl to Jonah. It isn't like she is in danger. Go! Go to your great-grandparents.*

Emmaline pushed harder against the ground with her feet, willing her mind to be calm, silently hushing the louder, panicked thoughts, clearing the way for the calmer, sweet, simple words floating there in her mind, and then she spoke them aloud, more to herself than to Mr. Tally.

She said, "I won't choose. Every bit of the story matters. It isn't mine to choose."

And then she looked down at the ground, and she remembered the apple Cecille had tried to give to the other storychanger, and she thought to herself...*I wonder.*

"You don't have to choose either." Emmaline spoke softly, kindly.

"What?" his voice was raspy, and sounded more like a grunt than a word.

"I said, you don't have to choose. You could just stand here, and maybe, just let things happen as they will, while I go dispose of the note. You don't have to change anything."

"This will end in a race, a battle of will and strength, and mine are strong," the storychanger said. "I won't just stand here."

"You could, though. You don't have to battle anything out." Her voice remained steady and calm.

Mr. Tally covered his ears, he leaned his head to the side, and his eyes squeezed shut, and it was clear he was in pain. He looked like someone who had been taken over by a violent earache.

And then Emmaline knew that kindness hurt these people. She had figured out something about this world, about this role, without Susannah or Jimmy telling her, and this made her feel like she was a little taller, a little more powerful than she had been only a moment ago. She had known all along that she had been on the right side of the story, but now she realized that not only was goodness on her side, but also that the other side was against goodness. Kindness itself pained those working on the wrong side, and suddenly, Emmaline felt terribly sad for storychangers. That must be the most awful of roles to play, Emmaline thought, the most lonely and treacherous way to live. She did not want to hurt anyone. If only everyone could be kind and good, she thought, tears prickling her eyes. She took a deep breath, carefully considering her words to stay true to the story, and also trying not to cause pain.

"I don't think I want to argue with you. And I think Jonah will still go to the fireworks. He seems like a hopeful kind of guy, or at least not the kind to miss out on a fireworks show on his first night in a new country. And I won't chase you. I think Jimmy has a good start. No, I'm playing offense now, I think. Defense time has come to an end."

And here she laughed a soft laugh and thought about Jimmy running down the street triumphantly, knowing the story had a plan and that he was working on the right side of it. He would be so pleased as he ran, Emmaline knew.

She looked back up at the storychanger, into his unreadable face, and her laughter died down. She could not laugh and look at someone with such a sad, dark existence. And then a single tear rolled down her cheek.

But then she cleared her throat, because while it was good to stand up for what was right, it was also good to be kind. "I could play by your rules, but I won't. And you don't have to either."

And then the man in front of her seemed to break, for his face crumbled in pain, his hands still pushing against his ears, and his face twisted into a grimace. But his eyes, those eyes that had seemed so terrible and dark in the jewelry shop, widened and seemed to lighten just a bit, as if he was considering something new. But then, as soon as Emmaline had noticed the change, it vanished, and the same stony, eerie gaze that had been in Mr. Tally's eyes back in the jewelry shop had returned.

He let out a terrific groan, and he reached into his pocket, pulled out a small glass jar with a candle inside. Its flame mysteriously burned, although it was inside a closed vessel. He twisted the lid until it opened, and he blew out the candle. As the flame went out, all of the holes that had been burned into the ground closed back up, and he, too, disappeared.

Emmaline breathed out the sigh that she hadn't had time to breathe out before this second encounter with the storychanger. And just as she started to smooth her skirt before heading in the direction of the fireworks, where she hoped she would find Jimmy, Cecille, and her great-grandparents, she felt as if the ground fell out from beneath her.

Chapter Fifteen

The *Story*

Emmaline was in the white room. The perfectly white, comfortable, lovely Place of Stillness, and Susannah was there.

"You did well."

"Where is Cecille?"

"With her family."

Emmaline took a deep breath and then let it out.

"Where is Jimmy?"

"I suspect he is resting, too," Susannah said, smiling. "You did well," she said again.

"Did what well? It's over? I didn't really do anything. I don't even know what I did, really. Just found a little girl sitting under a tree. I didn't even see her get to her uncle, my great-grand...Jonah, I mean."

"Believe me, you did well, Emmaline. Remember, this isn't your story; this is *the* story, and the smallest thing can make so many amazing and wonderful and important things happen as they should. Would you believe me, Emmaline," Susannah spoke, pulling out a set of brightly colored marbles from a velvet bag sitting beside her on the white ground, "if I told you that you stopped seventeen terrible things from happening today? Would you believe me," she said placing the marbles gently in a circle on the floor, "if I told you that today you made sure that no fewer than twenty important inventions would be made in time to save the lives of three pilots, and that you inspired the mind of a future teacher who would one day inspire the minds of hundreds of children to do thousands of wonderful things? And would you believe me, too, Emmaline, if I told you that you did help your great-grandmother to meet your great-grandfather, for without you, she would never have gone to that front door, and Jonah could not have later recognized the girl he had been smitten with standing there at the lemon ice cart?" Susannah smiled as she knocked one of the marbles out of place with another. "It seems you did get to play the role of—what was it—fairy great-granddaughter, after all." Susannah smiled.

"All that? How did I do all that?"

"You simply were willing to do what you felt was right. That's all it takes, Emmaline. We don't always have to understand. Being successful has so much more to do with being the one to stand up and say, 'I'll do this. I'll do something good. I may not know exactly how or why or what, but I'll try, and I'll listen.' Do you understand what I'm saying, Emmaline?"

"Yes." Emmaline laughed and shook her head, "Well, no."

"I'm saying you are a storysmith, and you did a wonderful job, and you'll never know exactly everything you did, though I imagine you may find some clues in one of those history books of yours." And now Susannah laughed. Then her face suddenly turned serious, and she said, "It's time to go back. Hold tight to that ring. It's your connection to the storysmiths before you, to your role here and in other times."

"Okay, I will," Emmaline said, and then, "thank you."

"That's what friends are for," Susannah said. And then she scooped the beautiful set of marbles into her hand and dropped them into the velvet bag. "Here," she said, holding the bag out to Emmaline.

"What are these for?"

"For playing marbles, silly. We used to play with them on the playground at school, and on the sidewalk outside your house."

"Oh, I know. I just thought…"

"That maybe they were magical marbles?" Susannah flashed a little smile.

Emmaline laughed, "Maybe."

"Well, maybe they are. I would get myself a leather satchel if I were you, and keep your storysmithing treasures in it. You never know if you may need them." Susannah smiled.

"Why a leather one?"

"A leather bag blends in much better in different times than, say, a neon plastic bag, don't you think?"

"That makes sense," Emmaline said.

Then the white walls, ceiling, and floor of the Place of Stillness faded away and the friends were standing on a grassy field. A flock of blackbirds stood in a circle around them. Emmaline was uneasy, even with Susannah beside her, for the blackbirds had, until then, seemed to appear at troublesome moments, and she wasn't sure where they fit into this storysmithing business or why they were here now. But, Susannah seemed delighted to see them. "These are wonderful birds. They had only been used for darkness, but now, they have been made good, and they are ready to take you on an adventure. A sort of recasting for them, shall we say?"

Emmaline looked at the birds, surprised that she no longer found them creepy. Now they looked beautiful, black and shining and majestic. A beautiful woven carpet of purple and crimson and Emmaline's very favorite shade of grass green appeared beneath her feet, Susannah moved away from her, whispering, "Goodbye. For now."

The birds gathered around the edges of the carpet, took hold of it in their beaks, began to flap their obsidian wings, and they rose in flight, taking Emmaline and the beautiful carpet up with them. She was standing on a flying carpet! And she laughed, for it was possibly the least sensible thing that she could have ever imagined, yet, it felt so wonderfully right. The flight was smooth and steady, so much so that she felt no need to sit down.

Emmaline, now somewhat changed herself, raised her hands out to her sides and imagined that she, too, was a blackbird, soaring gracefully through magical, storybook realms. And, together they flew, into the light blue, cloudless sky, and it was absolutely wonderful. She closed her eyes for only a moment, and when she opened them, she was standing on the ground in the front yard of her grandfather's farm house, her arms still raised. The carpet and the birds had disappeared, but Emmaline Hazeltree still felt that she was flying, for she had been on a truly marvelous adventure, and really, she couldn't wait to start on another one, whenever that may be.

The End

Epilogue

Ending Happily

It had been a summer full of ordinary things. There had been chickens to feed, dishes to wash, and sunsets to see. But Emmaline found all of those things full of wonder as she sat in the evenings with her grandfather, out on his front porch, he quietly rocking while his old rocking chair squeaked, and she reclining against the porch rail, her legs stretched out in front of her, across the top step of the porch. She realized then, on those quiet evenings on the farm, that everything was a part of the story, that she was a character, that life was an adventure, and that while sometimes there may be dragons to slay and treasures to find, other times, there would be stillness to take comfort in or orange sunsets to watch until they turned to dark violet. Some evenings, out on that porch, she thought of her parents, and she wondered if they had worked things out between them, and if her family would all stay together in the same house after the end of the summer. Sometimes she cried, thinking that maybe they were splitting up forever. Other nights, she hoped; she hoped with a fierceness that nearly took her breath away. And there were evenings that summer when she would look up at her solemn, kind grandfather who had no idea where she had been, but seemed to know it was somewhere good, and he would look down at her and nod, nearly smiling, but not quite, and she realized that there wasn't much she could do to change the story. She could only work with it, follow it where it led, and listen. She realized that she could play only her role, and she couldn't make anyone else's choices for them. Although she could hope and advise and listen and help, the story was the story. And whether her parents' story went this way or another way, they were still her parents, and her parents loved her, and the story they all lived in was still *the* story. And if the details didn't all fit smoothly and happily into place, the story's theme would always play out as it should in the end. Because, she knew, in the world of this story, it was already written that good always wins. And this made her feel warm and content inside. Looking at her grandfather and at the farm surrounding his front porch, listening to the cicadas, smelling the cut grass, and thinking that the story had already been written, gave her so much peace, that at times she felt she was back in the Place of Stillness with Susannah, with that warm contented feeling letting her know that all would be well. She always had loved stories, but now she found them in the world around her, not just in books.

That wasn't to say that Emmaline did not still love books. She did, and on the occasion of her returning home at the end of the summer, the very first thing she did was race up her stairs—which, she noticed, had larger steps than those built more than one hundred years ago—throw open her bedroom door, and drop down on her knees before her tidy stacks of books where she began pulling out history volumes and searching hurriedly through their pages. In the third history book she pulled out, a small vanilla-and-earth smelling book with a green canvas cover, she found what she had hoped to find. She found a name, Cecille Hazeltree. It was in the index, and beside it were the words, "inventor, scientist, physician, page 75."

With trembling fingers, Emmaline turned to page 75 where she learned four things about Cecille Hazeltree: She was lost from her parents for years after a terrible ship wreck, but then reconciled to them with the help of her uncle who miraculously found her in a chance encounter. She was admitted to medical school at the age of seventeen. And she loved to design and fly her own airplanes. Her greatest achievement was in her tireless efforts to make both education and comfort available to children who otherwise would have had neither.

Until that moment, Emmaline Hazeltree had never realized that even history books can have happy endings. Emmaline reached up for a pencil from her desk, and she scribbled a few words in the margin above the section on Cecille Hazeltree.

"Once upon a time…" she wrote, thinking that there really was no role she would rather have than that of a storysmith.